RIDING FOR THE STARS

Also by Maggie Dana

Keeping Secrets, Timber Ridge Riders (Book 1)
Racing into Trouble, Timber Ridge Riders (Book 2)
The Golden Horse of Willow Farm, Weekly Reader Books
Remember the Moonlight, Weekly Reader Books
Best Friends series, Troll Books

TIMBER RIDGE RIDERS
∾ Book Three ∾

RIDING FOR THE STARS

Maggie Dana

PAGEWORKS PRESS

ISBN 978-0-9851504-2-6

Edited by Judith Cardanha
Cover by Margaret Sunter
Interior design by Anne Honeywood
Published by Pageworks Press
Text set in Sabon

for Nancy and Eli
because they are stars!

(and because Eli likes carrots as much as Magician does)

1

HOLLY CHAPMAN LET OUT A YELP. The book she'd been reading fell to the floor with a thunk. "I don't believe it," she said. "This is such a cop-out."

Kate McGregor glanced at her friend. "What's wrong?"

Holly's nose had been stuck in the latest *Moonlight* book since before dinner. She'd even forgotten to eat her buttercrunch ice cream, now melting in a glass bowl on the nightstand between their two beds.

"He's a *vampire*," Holly said.

"Who?"

"Warrior."

"But that's the horse, isn't it?" Kate hadn't read any of the *Moonlight* books, but she'd learned enough about the characters from Holly's elaborate descriptions to know that Warrior wasn't human. He was just an ordinary black stallion who happened to be three hundred years old and able to leap tall buildings in a single bound.

"Exactly," Holly said. "Horses can't be vampires, can they?"

Kate bared her teeth. "Only if they bite you."

"Stop making fun."

The *Moonlight* series was Holly's favorite. It was filled with time-traveling teens, magical horses, and a pale-faced heroine named Ophelia Brown, who always seemed to be fleeing from something dark and sinister. Kate preferred *Dressage Today*. She'd just read an article about creating checkerboard patterns on a show horse's rump and couldn't wait to try it out on Buccaneer, the barn's newest horse. He had the perfect coat.

Holly said Kate needed to lighten up.

Kate told Holly to get a grip on reality.

From the depths of her pony print comforter, Holly pulled out the latest issue of *Seventeen*. She ripped off its plastic wrapper and began to turn pages. Moments later, she let out another yelp.

"What now?" Kate said.

"I know something you don't," Holly said in a stage whisper. "About the movie."

"*Moonlight?*"

Holly rolled her eyes. "What else?"

It had already turned their lives upside down. Instead of practicing for the next horse show, the riding team was now focused on *Moonlight* because part of it was to be filmed at Timber Ridge Stables. Copies of the book had erupted all over the barn. One of the girls was reading it on a smart phone. Another had her nose glued to an iPad.

Then the movie's director, who owned Buccaneer, had caused even more excitement by announcing that one of the barn's riders would be chosen as a stunt double for the film's female lead.

Kate desperately wanted the job—all the girls did. They wanted the glamour, the excitement of being in a film, and a few heady moments of fame. All Kate wanted was enough money to buy a horse of her own. The latest rumor said the stunt double would be paid a thousand dollars.

"Okay," said Kate. "What *about* the movie?"

So far, Hollywood had kept a tight lip about the movie's lead role, and every *Moonlight* fan in the world had been waiting for news, including Holly.

She scrambled off her bed, threw herself onto Kate's, and slapped down the magazine. "Ta-dah!"

A full-page photo of Tess O'Donnell.

Kate stared at the picture. Tess O'Donnell had masses of blond hair, a 4.0 average, and offers from Ivy League colleges that couldn't wait to scoop her up when she graduated from high school next year. Tess starred in Holly's favorite TV show, and her name had been connected with every teen idol since Aladdin.

"So?" Kate said.

"She's got the part."

For a moment, it didn't compute.

What part? Kate wondered. Then the penny dropped. "You mean Tess O'Donnell's going to play Ophelia Brown?"

Holly sighed. "She will be *so* perfect."

Kate looked at the photo again. Standing beside a chestnut with droopy ears, Tess O'Donnell wore a ruffled denim shirt, white breeches, and a nervous expression, like she'd never been that close to a horse before.

"Can she actually ride?" Kate asked.

There was a slight pause. "No, but—"

"That's dumb," Kate said. "They should find someone else."

"Who cares if Tess can't ride," Holly said. "One of us will be doing it for her." She clasped the magazine to her chest. "I just hope it's not Princess Angela."

Kate pulled a face. Angela Dean would probably win the stunt-double role by default. Her parents were friends with Giles Ballantine, the movie's director. Kate had been riding his horse for a month but had never actually met him. According to Liz, Holly's mom, who ran the stables, Giles Ballantine was a wealthy celebrity who didn't know one end of a horse from the other.

"What about the close-ups?" Kate said. "You can't fake those."

Holly shrugged. "Tess will ride a pretend horse."

"It won't fool anybody," Kate said, remembering the mechanical racehorses in the movie of *Seabiscuit*. Even Holly had laughed at them.

"Most people don't know beans about horses," Holly said. "They won't know it's a fake." She flipped her blond pony tail, snatched up her book, and struck a pose—one hand on her hip, the other brandishing *Moonlight*.

Kate grinned at her best friend—the first one she'd ever had.

The girls at her old riding stable in Connecticut weren't really friends; they just rode horses together. Then, this summer, her dad had gone to Brazil on a field trip and sent Kate to Vermont to stay with his sister. Aunt Marion was great, but after a week with nothing to do, Kate was bored out of her mind. So she got a job helping Holly, who was then still in a wheelchair, and now she couldn't imagine life without her.

They argued about almost everything—clothes, books, makeup, boys—but never about horses. They both adored Magician, Holly's gelding, and agreed that Buccaneer, who loved to eat peppermint Life Savers, was the coolest horse in the barn.

The best part, though, was watching Holly in action now, doing ordinary stuff that everyone else took for granted—jumping in and out of bed, picking up a book, or something as simple as just walking across their room and banging on the bathroom door because Kate was taking too long in the shower.

Two years ago, when Holly was twelve, she'd been in a car accident that killed her father and left her unable to walk or even stand by herself. The docs called it hysterical paralysis. There was nothing wrong with Holly's legs; it was all in her mind. It had locked itself up and thrown away the key. But another accident—a recent barn fire—had unlocked it, and Holly was now back to walking again. She was also riding her horse. Tomorrow, she would take another big step forward by jumping him.

"Are you excited?" Kate said.

"About the movie?"

"No, silly. About jumping Magician."

Holly set down her book. "I'm scared witless."

"Scared?" Kate said. "You're the bravest person I know."

"I'm a total wimp."

"Yeah, right," Kate said. "You only saved Buccaneer's life."

He was in the barn by himself when a fire broke out. Holly was there alone. No cell phone, nobody to call on for help. So Holly had forced herself out of her wheelchair. She'd gotten up and walked for the first time in two years, and she'd pulled Buccaneer to safety.

People ooh'd and aah'd, and the local papers made a big fuss. Buccaneer's owner sent two dozen white roses and a generous check, but Holly sent the check back. She said that being able to walk again was reward enough.

For a moment, both girls were silent.

Then Holly said, "Being brave doesn't mean you can't be scared. I'm scared lots of times. I'm scared of failure, scared of messing up, and—"

"Magician won't let you mess up," Kate said, trying to lighten their mood. "He took over my dressage test when I forgot it, remember?"

Holly still teased her about it. At the last show, Kate had blanked out the moment she entered the arena.

Nerves, probably. She didn't know which way to turn, but Magician did. He'd memorized the dressage test better than Kate had.

"You're right." Holly let out a sigh. "My horse is brilliant. Just keep reminding me of that, okay?"

* * *

Kate cheered when Holly and Magician jumped the crossrail. It was only two feet—much lower than the jumps Holly used to take. Before the accident, Holly had been a star rider. She and Magician had won ribbons and trophies at shows all over New England. She'd even been tagged as a Young Rider candidate.

"Way to go, Holly," Liz called out.

Kate cupped her mouth with both hands. "Epic!" she yelled.

"I never thought this would happen," Liz said, sounding choked up. "I never thought Holly would ever walk again, let alone ride and jump." With her easy smile, tousled blond hair, and vivid blue eyes, Liz Chapman looked young enough to be Holly's sister rather than her mother.

Grinning hugely, Holly trotted toward them.

"You guys looked awesome," Kate said.

Holly had been riding Magician every day since she got back on her feet, but this was the first time Liz had allowed her to jump. Kate ran a hand down the gelding's arched neck. He was a deep, dark brown—so dark, he was almost black, the color of a wet seal—and he didn't have a speck of white anywhere.

Holly shrugged. "Kid stuff."

"Just take it easy, okay?" Liz said. "No crazy stunts."

"Spoilsport," Holly said, still grinning.

Liz pinned her with a look. "Promise?"

"Okay, Mom," Holly said, winking at Kate. "I'll save the Olympics for next week."

Kate tried to put herself in Holly's shoes. *What did it feel like to be riding her own horse again?* Kate couldn't begin to imagine, but she knew how thrilled Holly was. Her legs were still a bit unreliable and didn't always do what she wanted, but they were getting stronger every day, thanks to a vigorous exercise program that included two hours of swimming, an hour in the saddle, and many miles on a treadmill.

"I have to get back to work," Liz said, patting her daughter's scuffed riding boot. "Can I trust you to behave yourself out here?"

"Cross my heart," Holly said.

"Just don't cross your fingers as well," warned her mother, before heading off to the barn.

Magician nudged Kate with his nose.

"Do you want to ride him?" Holly said. "I'm really beat."

"Sure," Kate said. She'd hardly ridden Holly's horse since Buccaneer came to the barn. His arrival coincided with Liz injuring her ankle, so Kate had taken over all his training. He was a willful, spirited horse, but he had a soft spot for Kate. Holly said it was because Kate bribed him with Life Savers.

Holly slid awkwardly off Magician's back. Her legs crumpled as she hit the ground. "Yikes," she said. "That hurts."

"Are you okay?"

"I'm stiff and sore, and my thighs are screaming for mercy," Holly said. "But it feels wonderful." Reaching up, she grabbed Kate's hand and lurched to her feet, then collapsed onto an upturned muck bucket. "Take Magician over the whole course. I love watching him jump."

"You sure he's not too tired?"

"My horse never gets tired," Holly said. "He's the Energizer Bunny Horse." She pulled off her helmet and body protector and handed them to Kate, then yanked off her scrunchie. "Take this as well. Your hair's a mess."

Kate scooped up her thick brown hair and tied it back. Holly's helmet was a little loose, but the body protector fit her slender frame perfectly. She fastened its straps and swung herself into the saddle. Magician was raring to go. Holly had warmed him up nicely.

After circling at a trot and slow canter, Kate aimed Magician at the parallel bars. As he soared over them, Kate leaned into his flying mane and realized how lucky she was, riding Magician and living at Timber Ridge with Holly and Liz. On top of all that, she got to train an amazing horse like Buccaneer and hang out with other girls who loved horses as much as she did.

It was the best thing that ever happened to her.

Kate circled Magician again and was about to jump the hogsback—a fearsome spread of red-and-white poles—when she spotted another horse and rider entering the ring. Her good mood vanished. *Why did Angela Dean have to show up and ruin a fabulous afternoon?*

As usual, Angela was perfectly turned out—tan breeches, crisp yellow shirt, and highly polished black boots. Her horse was highly polished, too. It looked as if someone had sprayed his dark bay coat with varnish.

Kate jumped the hogsback, but her heart wasn't in it any more. Angela's unexpected arrival had taken the fun out of things. Kate gave Magician a loose rein and rejoined Holly, still sitting on the muck bucket. She was staring at Angela, now trotting in circles on the wrong diagonal.

Holly gave a snort of disgust. "I wonder who she got to buff him up this time."

It was an old joke. Angela hated any kind of dirty work and always found someone else to groom her horse or clean her tack.

"What do you suppose is going on?" Kate said. "Angela never rides without an audience."

"Maybe she's just showing off for us," Holly said.

"I don't think so," Kate said, pointing. "Look over there."

A silver Mercedes was pulling up to the barn. Doors opened and out stepped Angela's mother wearing a flowered dress and high heels. With her was a man Kate didn't know.

But it had to be Giles Ballantine, the movie director.

Who else would wear Hollywood-sized sunglasses, a ten-gallon hat, and bright red cowboy boots in the middle of Vermont?

2

"QUICK," HOLLY SAID. "Let's put Magician in his stall, then we can come back and watch Angela showing off."

"Or falling off," Kate said.

Holly winced. She hated it when riders fell off, but Angela had deserved it. The day after Buccaneer arrived, she'd ridden him without permission and sawed at his mouth like a lumberjack. So he bucked her off. Angela promptly blamed Kate, who'd been schooling Buccaneer, by spreading the rumor that Kate had riled him up on purpose just so Angela would get dumped.

It was all part of Angela's campaign to get rid of Kate.

Holly had known Angela since kindergarten, and she hadn't changed a bit from the spoiled five-year-old who

13

threw a tantrum if another kid got gold stars and she didn't. The stakes were higher now, the prizes much bigger, and Angela wanted them all. At the last horse show, she'd put the riding team at risk by cheating her way to the individual gold medal. A week later, Angela turned the facts inside out and pointed the finger of blame at Kate.

So far, her tactics hadn't worked. Kate was still at Timber Ridge, she was the team's best rider, and Holly intended for it to stay that way.

* * *

Clutching her cell phone, Liz met them in the barn. "Mrs. Dean called. She's bringing Giles Ballantine over."

"We just saw him," Holly said, as Kate got off Magician and handed her the reins. "Sunglasses the size of headlamps and a hat you could take a bath in."

"He wants to see Kate ride Buccaneer," her mother said.

"Does he want to see Angela ride as well?"

Liz frowned. "I don't think so. Why?"

"Because she's out there, too," Kate said.

"Then keep out of her way," Liz said. "There's plenty of room for both of you." She pocketed her cell phone. "Now hustle. He's an impatient man."

Holly led Magician into his stall. She pulled off his saddle and threw a cooler over his back. For a moment, she leaned against him and soaked up his warmth. She ached from head to toe. Even her eyelashes hurt, but Holly didn't care. Being able to feel pain was a treasure. For two years, she'd been numb from the waist down, but now all the leg muscles she owned—and a few she didn't even know she owned—were reminding her they were part of her body.

Holly looked down at her feet. She lifted one foot and wiggled it, then wiggled the other.

Amazing!

She was still a little shocked when her legs obeyed instructions. Everyone else took this for granted—you tell your body to do something and, unless you're asking the impossible, your body performs.

More or less.

That morning, she'd announced over breakfast that she wanted to try out for the stunt-double role. Kate gave her a high-five, but Mom had choked on her granola.

"No way, Holly," she said. "Not this time. You're doing great with Magician, but you're nowhere near ready for something like this. I'd never forgive myself if you got hurt again."

They argued, and Holly lost.

An impossible dream—Holly knew that—but she had to try. If you didn't try, then nothing happened and you stopped believing in yourself. And if you stopped believing in yourself, it meant you were ready to give up.

Holly shook her head. She would never give up.

She removed Magician's bridle and wiped off his bit—a thick, rubber snaffle—then ran her hands down his shoulder. He was still warm. He needed to be walked out, but her exhausted legs couldn't cope. Normally, Kate would cool him off, but she was tacking up Buccaneer and getting ready to ride.

Jennifer West, the barn's newest rider, popped her head over Magician's stall door. She'd once been Angela's best friend until Angela badmouthed Kate all over Facebook and Twitter and Jennifer had wised up.

"Need help?" she said.

"Yes," Holly said. "Can you cool him off for me?"

"Sure," Jennifer said. "No problem." She snapped a leadrope onto Magician's halter.

Jennifer's nails were painted ten different shades of purple, and her short, spiky hair was bright orange. Yesterday, it was plain old brown. The week before, it had been strawberry blond. Her horse, Rebel, loved to eat vanilla pudding.

"Thanks," Holly said. "I owe you."

In the aisle, Buccaneer snorted and danced sideways as Kate struggled to tighten his girth. His long, black mane rippled in waves down his muscular neck; his tail almost touched the ground. Kate had changed into her own helmet and body protector, but she still wore the stained t-shirt and patched breeches she'd had on all day.

Holly hoped the director wouldn't notice.

* * *

Kate slipped a couple of Life Savers to Buccaneer and took him outside. Holly held his bridle while Kate mounted. The black gelding jigged about like a jack-in-the-box as if he knew that this was a watershed moment.

"Where's Magician?" Kate said.

"Jen's got him," Holly said. "She's cooling him off."

"In the ring?"

"No, in the back paddock."

Kate let out a sigh of relief. It was bad enough having Skywalker in the ring. Having Magician there as well would send Buccaneer into orbit. He performed much better on his own, with no other horses to distract him. Last week he'd refused to jump because two kids on ponies were practicing for the next gymkhana. He wanted to join their apple-bobbing race more than he wanted to jump the parallel bars.

Holly adjusted Kate's stirrups. "Are you nervous?"

"Yup."

"You'll be fine," Holly said. "Just remember that Mr. Movie Director doesn't know one end of a horse from another."

"But what if—?"

"Go," Holly said. "They're waiting."

Kate gathered up her reins and walked Buccaneer into the ring. Liz was already there, talking to Mrs. Dean and Giles Ballantine, who'd removed his hat and was now fanning himself with it. Buccaneer kept a wary eye on the flapping Stetson. He tossed his head and refused to go any closer. Kate tightened her grip. If she didn't watch out, he'd spook and take off with her.

Mrs. Dean applauded as her daughter popped Skywalker over the crossrail. "That's lovely, dear," she said. "Now, why don't you jump the bigger ones? Show Uncle Giles what you can do."

Uncle?

Kate could hear Holly giggling behind her.

Angela and Skywalker thundered by. The bay gelding had already worked up a sweat, and Angela had him on such a tight rein he was fighting the bit. They trotted over the brush jump, not much higher than the crossrail, then turned around and jumped it from the other direction.

"Why isn't she jumping the high ones?" Mrs. Dean said.

Liz laid a hand on her arm and said something. Kate couldn't hear the words, but from the expression on Mrs. Dean's face, it was obvious she didn't like what she was hearing. She shook off Liz's hand.

"I bet you anything Mom's telling her that Angela shouldn't jump," Holly whispered.

"Why?" Kate said. "She's jumped all these before."

"Yeah, but look at Skywalker. He's in a foul mood. His ears are pinned, and his tail's swishing back and forth like an angry cat. He's about to blow a gasket."

"So is Angela," Kate said.

Beneath her black helmet, Angela's face was starkly white, her mouth a grim line. She looked defiant and scared. Skywalker was pretty much a push-button horse. Push the right ones and he performed. But today he was anything but push-button, and Angela couldn't cope.

For a moment, Kate felt desperately sorry for her.

It was Mrs. Dean's fault. She pushed Angela to win, no matter the cost. If it wasn't a horse show, it was ski racing or a tennis tournament. Last week Angela was runner-up in the club's junior singles match, but she got yelled at for not trying harder.

Halfway down the ring, Angela skidded Skywalker to a halt. Gobs of foam flew from his mouth and landed on his sweaty neck like tiny marshmallows. Angela jerked him around, dug in her spurs, and headed for the hogsback. Dirt and stones flew from Skywalker's shiny hooves as he gathered speed.

"Angela, no!" Liz yelled. "Pull away."

But Angela kept going. She flicked her whip across Skywalker's rump. He lengthened his stride, and Angela threw herself forward, arms stretched up his neck. He stumbled, took an extra step, and corkscrewed over the jump so violently that Angela almost fell off. She was barely hanging on when they landed on the other side amid crashing poles.

Kate gasped. "Ouch, that must hurt."

"Yeah," Holly said. "Especially with her mother watching."

"*And* Mr. Ballantine." Kate glanced at the movie director, but he didn't appear the least bit fazed by Angela's colossal flub-up. He was more focused on Kate and Buccaneer, and it made Kate all the more nervous.

Suppose she made a worse mess than Angela? Buccaneer could easily refuse to jump. He'd been a beast yesterday. Hadn't done a thing Kate asked of him. She'd finally given up and gone trail riding with Jennifer and Rebel instead.

Giles Ballantine ambled toward her, thumbs tucked into his belt loops like an old-time gunslinger. Kate half expected him to pull out a six-shooter.

"You must be Kate McGregor," he said.

"Howdy, pardner," Holly whispered.

Kate stifled a nervous giggle as Giles Ballantine held out his massive hand. She leaned down to shake it. It was like being grasped by a grizzly bear

"Liz has told me great things about you," he said, smiling, "She says you've done wonders with my horse."

Kate felt herself blush. "Thanks."

Amid beard and mustache, the movie director's teeth glowed magnificently white. His bushy eyebrows stuck up like a hedge behind his enormous sunglasses. Kate could see herself reflected in the lenses.

"Okay, it's time for some *real* action," Giles Ballantine said. He patted Buccaneer's neck, then bounced his hand off Kate's riding boot. "Let's see if you guys can do any better."

Behind her, Kate heard an angry gasp.

She turned and met Angela's pale blue eyes, boring into her like lasers. No matter how much Kate wanted the stunt-double role, she knew that Angela wanted it even more. From now on, they'd be locked in a fierce rivalry that wouldn't end till Giles Ballantine chose the girl who would ride for Tess O'Donnell.

Buccaneer flicked his ears and pranced sideways.

"Easy boy," Kate said.

Holly gave her a thumbs-up. "Hang in there."

Kate nodded, then steered her fractious horse away from the jumps. She needed to warm him up, get him to pay attention and accept the bit. Right now, Buccaneer wasn't fit to jump the crossrail, never mind the parallel bars or the hogsback.

* * *

"What's she doing?" Giles Ballantine said. "Why isn't she jumping like the other girl did?"

Other girl?

Holly bit back a smile and plunked herself down on the muck bucket. Giles Ballantine didn't appear to know Angela quite as well as she pretended he did. "Kate's warming him up," Holly said, rubbing her sore thighs. "With a little dressage."

"What's that?"

"It's a French word for 'training.'"

After watching Kate and Buccaneer perform a brilliant extended trot and a passable shoulder-in, Holly glanced at her mother. She was still corralled by Mrs. Dean and no doubt getting an earful about Angela's shoddy performance. Beside them, Angela slouched in Skywalker's saddle and shot venomous looks at Kate, now cantering Buccaneer over the brush jump.

"That's better," said Giles Ballantine. "We're finally getting somewhere." He rubbed his hands gleefully, like a toddler with a shiny new truck.

Kate turned Buccaneer toward the chicken coop, and Holly crossed her fingers. The willful horse loved to jump, but only when he felt like it. Three strides later, he gathered himself up and soared over the coop like a big, black bird. Another two strides, and he cleared the parallel bars with room to spare.

Holly let out her breath, unaware she'd been holding it.

"Good," Giles Ballantine said, nodding vigorously. "Will she jump that one as well?" He pointed toward the hogsback that Liz had just put back together again. "How high is it?"

"Four feet," Holly said. "With a three-foot spread."

"Can horses jump higher?"

23

"Much," Holly said. "The record is eight feet."

Giles Ballantine gave a low whistle. "Boy, I'd love to see that."

A dozen questions tumbled through Holly's mind. She wanted to ask him about the movie. When was the screen test, what scenes would they shoot at Timber Ridge, and would Tess O'Donnell be part of it? But, most important of all, who'd be playing Ian Hamilton, the high school hottie who kept rescuing Ophelia Brown from one disaster after another?

Would it be Nathan Crane, her favorite actor?

* * *

Buccaneer cantered along the rail, skittering sideways like a crab. Kate softened her hands and sat deep in the saddle. Behind her, she could feel Buccaneer's tail swishing the way Skywalker's had done.

In the distance, something rumbled. Thunder?

No wonder her horse was acting up.

One more jump, and they'd be done. Kate slowed to a trot, then turned to look at the hogsback—three horizontal poles with the middle one higher than the two outside ones. It was set to exactly the same height as when she'd jumped it on Magician.

Except Buccaneer wasn't Magician.

He wasn't steady and predictable like Holly's reliable horse. With Buccaneer you never knew what would happen, especially when he was in a skittish mood. He could just as easily bound over a jump like a kangaroo or stop dead and you'd go flying over it without him.

Was it worth the risk?

Would jumping the stupid hogsback make any difference to her chances on the screen test? Kate glanced at her audience, standing in the middle of the ring and waiting for her next move.

Just then, a flash of lightning lit up the sky.

Raindrops the size of peas splattered onto Kate's bare arms. Down they came, faster and harder till they felt like bullets stinging her cheeks. She wiped them off and stared at the hogsback. It blurred before her eyes. In a few seconds, the jump's take-off zone would be a treacherous mess of puddles and mud.

Liz would kill her if she tried to jump it.

But Angela would scoff. She'd turn this into a victory.

3

HOLLY GAVE A SHUDDER of relief. She hated storms, but this one was a gift. It saved Kate from a bad decision. Ignoring her sore muscles, Holly ran for the gate. A vicious wind whipped through the ring. Leaves and twigs tore loose from the brush jump; an empty barrel rolled into a set of uprights.

Kate and Angela rode their horses directly into the barn.

The last Holly saw of Mrs. Dean, she was soaked and barefoot and complaining loudly because her legs were covered with mud. Giles Ballantine hustled her into the Mercedes and drove off.

Holly found Kate in Buccaneer's stall, rubbing him

down. Steam rose from the horse's wet rump. Rain pounded the barn's roof like a million tiny jackhammers.

"Well, that was exciting," Kate said.

"I'll say." Holly pushed a hunk of wet hair from her face. "Were you really going to jump the hogsback?"

There was a moment's hesitation.

Kate kept on brushing and wiping, and Holly had her answer. No way did Kate want to tackle that jump, and Holly didn't blame her. Not on Buccaneer, and not in the middle of a storm. He wouldn't be much good at the screen test either. He'd freak out for sure. Cameras and lights and clapperboards were way beyond his comfort zone.

Holly grabbed a cloth from Kate's grooming box and started on Buccaneer's other side. His ebony coat was a froth of sweat and mud. "Do you want Magician?"

"What for?" Kate said, looking up.

"The screen test."

"You're not going to try for it?"

"Nuh-uh, you heard what Mom said." Holly sighed. "But I guess she's right. I'd be stupid to risk getting hurt in the screen test and wreck my chances for the next team event."

"Wow," Kate said. "Are you sure?"

"You bet," Holly said.

"Then I'd love it."

"Cool," Holly said. "But there's one condition."

"What?"

"You've got to win!"

* * *

After Kate hot-walked Buccaneer in the indoor arena, she joined Holly in her mother's office. She glanced at the notice board above Liz's messy desk. Holly's comment about the next team event had brought back another worry—the Timber Ridge riding team.

There were four members when Kate first arrived. Now there were six, and everyone had her own horse, except Kate. She scanned the list:

Angela Dean—Skywalker

Robin Shapiro—Chantilly

Jennifer West—Rebel

Susan Piretti—Tara

Holly Chapman—Magician

Kate McGregor—Buccaneer

Trouble was, she wouldn't have Buccaneer much longer. His owner would be taking him away as soon as the movie stuff was finished. And there wasn't another horse in the barn that could take his place. She absolutely *had* to win the screen test.

"You look bummed out," Holly said, swiveling her mom's creaky old chair back and forth. "What's wrong?"

"Nothing."

"Come on," Holly said. "I'm your best friend, *remember*?"

Kate couldn't keep it to herself any longer. Holly would probably laugh and tell her she was dreaming. She sucked in her breath. "I'm gonna buy a horse."

"That's cool," Holly said. "But how? You don't have any money."

"I will if I win the screen test."

Holly stopped in mid-swivel. "But that's only a thousand bucks," she said. "It'll buy you both ears, one leg, and the tail."

"Horses don't have to be expensive."

"Good ones do," Holly said. "Sue's parents just paid five thousand for Tara, and Magician's worth way more than that."

Kate sighed. Holly wasn't exaggerating. Sue Piretti's pretty little mare was a steady jumper, but she was no match for Magician, or even Buccaneer.

29

"Have you told Mom?" Holly said.

"No."

"Why not?"

"She'll think I'm crazy," Kate said. "So keep it to yourself, okay? I don't want anyone to know."

"Especially Angela," Holly said. "If she finds out, it'll make her even more determined to beat you."

Kate looked at the list again. "Who else will try out?"

"*Everyone*," Holly said. "The whole riding team."

"But none of their horses match the story," Kate said, mentally running through the barn's horsy color scheme—dark bay, chestnut, dappled gray, and an Appaloosa. Only Buccaneer and Magician fitted Warrior's description.

"Unless Angela paints Skywalker black," Holly said.

"I wouldn't put it past her."

"Neither would I," Holly said. "But suppose she persuades Giles Ballantine to let her ride Buccaneer."

"She won't," Kate said. "She's terrified of him."

"Then you've got nothing to worry about."

* * *

The next day was blisteringly hot. After morning barn chores, Kate and Holly ran home and jumped into the

Chapmans' pool. While Holly swam laps, Kate lolled about on her back and gazed at Timber Ridge Mountain. Ski trails, lush with midsummer grass, spilled from its peak like dribbles of green paint. Kate had never learned to ski, but she'd ridden the lower trails with Buccaneer and Magician. That's where the cross-country course was.

Holly's cell phone chirped.

She was in the deep end, practicing flip turns, so Kate snagged the phone from their pile of towels. It was probably Adam Randolph—Holly's sort-of boyfriend—and Kate knew she wouldn't want to miss his call. But it was Liz calling from the barn.

Kate listened for a moment, then hung up.

Holly swam to the edge. "Was that Adam?"

"No. It was your Mom."

"Is everything okay?"

"Yeah," Kate said. "Mr. Ballantine wants us all to ride first thing tomorrow morning. Then he'll pick two of us to take a final screen test."

"When?"

"Next week." All of a sudden, Kate's confidence drained away, like somebody just pulled the plug. "Mr. Ballantine knows *nothing* about horses," she said. "It'll be a humongous disaster."

"No, it won't," Holly said. "You'll win. Easy, peasy."

But Kate wasn't so sure. What if Giles Ballantine changed the script to match whatever color horse took his fancy? Or worse—suppose Holly was right and Angela convinced him to let her ride Buccaneer? He'd be crazy not to choose his own horse.

* * *

Kate was up before dawn. She groomed Magician so hard, she could almost see her reflection in his dark, glossy coat. Then she trimmed his whiskers, oiled his hooves, and brushed his mane till it glistened. Holly had already cleaned his tack.

One by one, the other girls arrived. They carried buckets and grooming boxes and argued over who loved *Moonlight* the best. Their voices buzzed with excitement.

All except Angela's.

Kate checked Skywalker's stall. One of the younger kids was currying him; another sat on a tack trunk, rubbing soap into Angela's saddle and bridle. Marcia, Angela's younger sister, was combing the tangles from Skywalker's tail.

"Where's Angela?" Kate said.

Marcia looked up. "At home, getting ready."

"Typical," Holly muttered.

It was time to change. Kate wiped her hands on a rag and raced for the tack room. Jennifer, Sue, and Robin were already in there, exchanging jeans and grubby sneakers for buff breeches, Timber Ridge t-shirts, and well-polished black boots.

Liz had insisted they all wear the same thing. "This won't be a fashion parade," she said. "Mr. Ballantine will be looking at you and your horses, not your outfits."

By eight-forty-five, everyone was spit-shined and ready. Marcia and her minions had Skywalker all tacked up, waiting for his owner to arrive. Moments later, Mrs. Dean's silver Mercedes pulled into the parking lot. All eyes turned toward it.

"Angela's grand entrance," Holly muttered.

Doors opened. Out stepped Giles Ballantine wearing a baseball cap, denim overalls, and deck shoes. No socks, no sunglasses. At his side appeared a skinny young man with a clipboard and video camera. An assistant, Kate figured. Then came Mrs. Dean, followed by Angela.

Kate stared at her.

Had she gone completely nuts?

Instead of buff breeches and a green t-shirt, Angela was dressed entirely in white—breeches, shirt, helmet, and gloves. Even her boots were white. White ribbons fluttered from her shiny black hair, coiled neatly in a bun at the nape of her neck.

"Guess she missed Mom's lecture," Holly said.

Angela flashed a confident smile, as if this was just a formality, that she'd win the part, no questions asked. Then she mounted Skywalker and rode into the ring.

* * *

Magician and Kate didn't put a foot wrong. Neither did anyone else, including Angela and Skywalker. They walked, trotted, and cantered on cue. They did hand-gallops down the middle of the ring and jumped the fences that Giles Ballantine had chosen—the brush, parallel bars, and a modified hogsback.

With the big video camera on his shoulder, Giles Ballantine's assistant filmed them all, moving and standing still, in sunlight and shadow. He shot close-ups and wide-angle views—front, sideways, and rear. At one point, Kate was convinced he'd crawl between the horses' legs and shoot them from underneath.

The movie director made copious notes on his clipboard.

More than once, he conferred with Liz, who hadn't

said a word about Angela's dumb outfit. Maybe she'd bawl her out later—in private.

Holly said, "Mom probably doesn't care. She's just glad nobody has messed up." She grinned at Kate. "You guys did awesome. You'll win the screen test, for sure."

But they wouldn't find out till the next day.

4

THE NEWS THEY'D BEEN waiting for arrived by courier. He handed Kate a brown envelope and asked her to her sign for it. With trembling fingers, she ripped it open. Inside were three pages of script and a note with details about time and place.

Holly let out a whoop. "I knew you'd win."

Fighting back tears, Kate grabbed a kitchen chair and sat down hard. She read the note again. The screen test would be held in the barn's biggest meadow. It had practice jumps and an easy hunt course. The more challenging cross-country fences were nearby. "I wonder who else he chose."

"Angela, probably," Holly said. "Let me see the script."

She scanned the pages. "I know this scene," she said. "Ophelia's out trail riding, and she gets chased through a time portal by guys on motorbikes, and—"

"*Motorbikes?*"

"Yeah, and they turn into zombies on horseback."

"*Zombies?*" Kate gulped. "On horseback?"

"What did you expect?" Holly said. "Kittens on skateboards?"

"So, what does Ophelia turn into?" Kate said. This was getting hairier by the minute.

Holly grinned. "Read the book and find out."

* * *

Holly was right. By the time they got to the barn, it was bursting with the news that Kate and Angela were the two lucky winners. The other girls had received notes from the director, thanking them for trying out.

"I didn't expect to get it," Sue said, with a shrug. She wiped saddle soap off her hands and hung the bridle she'd been cleaning back on its hook.

Robin gave a wry grin. "Me neither."

"Besides," Jennifer said. "Our horses aren't the right color."

"Neither is Skywalker," Holly said.

"Doesn't matter," came another voice.

Angela Dean sauntered into the tack room. Her black Levis fitted like a second skin; her yellow crop-top had lace and tiny bows around the neck. Beneath one arm, she carried a brown envelope just like the one Kate had received.

"Why?" Kate said.

She stared at Angela's sandals. They matched her glossy red toenails and were exactly the sort of shoes you shouldn't wear in a horse barn.

"Because Uncle Giles is in charge," Angela said. "He can change the horse's color to anything he wants." She batted her eyelashes, heavy with mascara. "He thinks Skywalker is a perfect Warrior."

Holly snorted. "Yeah, right."

"Then I guess *Uncle* Giles thinks you're perfect, too." Robin held up the barn's tattered copy of *Moonlight*. "Ophelia's got black hair," she said. "I mean, it's seriously black."

"Just like mine," Angela said, patting hers. It framed her pale face like a pair of crow's wings.

"But Tess O'Donnell's a blonde," Jennifer said.

"With masses of curls," added Robin.

"Which means the director will probably change Ophelia's hair as well." Sue said. "From black to blond."

Angela shrugged. "Big deal."

"Does this mean you'll go blond and curly as well?" Holly said.

Kate smiled. She had visions of Angela going crazy with bleach and a curling iron. She'd once arrived for team practice with her hair in ringlets and gotten teased so bad, she didn't try it again. At least, not around the barn.

"Maybe," Angela said. "I'll discuss it with my hairdresser." She patted her hair again. "At *Salon de Cheveux.*"

"Isn't that French for 'horses?'" Robin said.

"That's *chevaux*, stupid," Angela retorted.

"Perfect," said Sue. "You can ask her to dye Skywalker as well."

"My grandmother tried that once," Jennifer said. "One of her favorite horses had a huge white blaze. It practically covered his face. Gran said it made him look like a cow, so she dyed it dark brown to match the rest of him."

"Did it work?"

"Yeah," Jennifer said. "Everything went great until it rained. Poor Gran. She was in the middle of a dressage test when it began to pour, and all the dye ran off her horse's face."

"That must've impressed the judges," Robin said,

laughing. She reached for her helmet. "Okay, who's coming for a trail ride?"

Everyone chimed in with a yes. Except Angela.

She'd retreated to the doorway and was leaning against it, clutching her script and trying to look as if she didn't care. Kate felt an unexpected surge of sympathy. She knew what it was like not to have friends. The girls at her old riding stable had expensive horses and wealthy parents. Kate worked there to earn her lessons. She mucked stalls, cleaned tack, and groomed horses. The other riders tolerated her because she made their team look good by winning blue ribbons.

"Come with us," she said.

There was a stunned silence.

Angela's face flushed pink. Her eyes glittered. Kate couldn't tell if it was tears or a trick of the light.

"I'm going to lunch," Angela finally said, pushing a strand of hair off her face. "With Uncle Giles."

In a flash, she was gone.

"Phew," Robin said. "That was a close one."

"Yeah," said Jennifer.

"Come on," Sue said. "Let's go riding."

They got busy with saddles and bridles and hunting down lost chaps. Loaded with gear, they left the tack room. Holly hung back. She grabbed Kate's arm.

"What *were* you thinking?"

"I felt sorry for her."

Holly snorted. "That's like feeling sorry for a crocodile that got heartburn because it ate a duckling."

* * *

From: Giles_Ballantine@gmail.com
To: Angela_Dean
Subject: Screen test
Wear comfortable riding clothes (prefer t-shirt and jeans or old breeches; nothing fancy), and please forward this to Kate McGregor. I don't have her e-mail address.

* * *

The night before her screen test, Kate panicked. Suppose Magician threw a shoe. Suppose it rained. Suppose she fell off and broke her arm.

What if Angela beat her?

"Chill out," Holly said. "You're driving me nuts."

Kate flopped onto her bed and stared at the ceiling. "What should I wear?"

"Didn't anyone tell you?"

Kate shook her head. "No."

Holly looked thoughtful. "How about lace?" she

said. "Or sequins and a feather boa?" Her eyes narrowed. "No, I've got it. You can wear Mom's old dressage stuff—shadbelly coat, yellow vest, top hat. The whole works. I bet she wouldn't mind."

"I'm serious," Kate said. "Help me out."

"Jeans and a t-shirt, then."

But all Kate could think about was Angela's white outfit. It was ridiculous and over-the-top, but it worked. Angela didn't ride any better than Jennifer or Robin or Sue, yet she won the screen test and they didn't.

Holly's cell phone chirped. It was probably Adam. Holly had spoken with him five times since dinner. She snuggled beneath her comforter the way she always did when he called late at night, then shot bolt upright again.

"You've *got* to be kidding," she said, glancing at Kate. "She wouldn't do *that*, would she?" There was a long pause. "Wow, you really aren't kidding."

All Kate's alarm bells rang at once. She scrambled off her bed and threw herself onto Holly's. Magazines and stuffed toys went flying. Books tumbled onto the floor. A tube of lip glass rolled off Holly's night table.

Holly flipped her phone from one ear to the other. "Yeah, uh-huh," she said. "I'll tell her. Call you back later. Bye."

"What?" Kate said.

"That was Jennifer," Holly said slowly. "She played tennis at the club this evening. Angela was there. They had a tournament, or something."

"So?" Kate said.

"Seems Angela went to the hairdresser."

Kate wanted to shake Holly till her teeth rattled, but she knew better than to push. Holly loved to spin out a story as long as possible. "Come on, tell me."

"She did it. I didn't think she had the guts, but—"

"Did what?" Kate said.

"Angela's gone blond," Holly said. "Blond and curly. Just like Tess O'Donnell."

* * *

An hour after Holly fell asleep, Kate was still wide awake. This was ridiculous, obsessing over a stupid screen test, but she couldn't help it. She needed that role. Angela didn't. She had a fabulous horse and parents with tons of money. All Kate had was an absentee father and a savings account with ninety bucks in it.

There had to be *something* she could do.

Clothes?

She'd wear her white breeches and a white cotton

shirt, maybe her navy hunt jacket. That ought to work. She'd look sharp and professional. No, scratch that. She'd be better off in jeans and a peasant blouse.

Kate fingered her hair, boring old brown and not even close to Tess O'Donnell's. Then a vision of Angela with blond curls swam into view.

Two could play at that game.

Without turning on the light, Kate climbed out of bed and fumbled her way to the bathroom. There was a bottle of hydrogen peroxide in the medicine cabinet. Liz used it for cuts and scrapes, but hairdressers used it, too—as bleach.

But did she dare do this?

Was she really that desperate? More to the point, did she have enough time? She glanced at her watch. One o'clock.

It would only take a few minutes.

In the end, it took ten, but nothing happened. Kate checked the directions. Nothing about using it on your hair. She sprayed and sprayed and dabbed with cotton balls—she used up the entire bottle—but her hair remained stubbornly mouse brown.

* * *

The alarm woke Holly at seven. For a moment, she just lay there, her mind racing in circles. This was Kate's big day, and Holly had promised to do everything she could to help. That's what best friends did for each other, even if one of them was just a little bit envious.

Holly sighed. She knew all about envy.

She'd spent two years being envious of people who could walk. Mom said envy was normal, especially when you're stuck in a wheelchair. It was jealousy that tore people apart and made them bitter. Angela was always jealous. It's why she didn't have any friends.

Holly yawned and stretched, then climbed out of bed. Kate was still asleep, completely buried in a tangle of sheets and blankets. Her left foot dangled free, hanging off the mattress. It was the only part of her Holly could see.

"Kate, wake up," Holly said.

No response. Not even a twitch.

"C'mon, Kate. If you don't get up now, I'll use all the hot water." She crossed the room and shook Kate's shoulder. They had less than two hours to muck stalls and groom horses and get themselves to the meadow by ten for the screen test.

"Go away," Kate mumbled.

Holly yanked off her covers. "Yikes!"

"What's wrong?" Kate struggled to sit up.

"Your hair," Holly said. She could barely get the words out. "It's . . . it's gone *yellow*."

Kate shoved her out of the way and stumbled into the bathroom. For a second or two, there was silence, then a ghastly noise, as if somebody was strangling a cat.

"Arrggggh," came Kate's voice.

Holly stuck her head around the door and snapped on the light. Kate's hair stuck out in all directions like the scarecrow in *The Wizard of Oz*. "What did you *do* to it?"

"That." Kate pointed to the peroxide bottle.

Holly shook it. Empty. "You used *all* of it?"

"Every last drop." Kate tugged at her hair, as if she wanted to pull it all out. "I'm an idiot, a moron. The stupidest girl in the world." She whipped around to face Holly, her face blotchy and streaked with tears. "I'm a freak."

"But why?" Holly said. "Why did you do this, and why did you do it without me?"

"You'd gone to sleep."

"You could've woken me up." Holly shook her head.

It didn't make sense. Kate loathed girly-girl stuff. She never wore makeup—not even lip gloss—and couldn't care less about clothes, unless it involved dressing up for a horse show. So why did she mess with her hair?

Suddenly, it fell into place. "*Angela?*"

"Who else?" Kate said.

"Let me get this straight," Holly said. "You bleached your hair because Angela did?"

"So shoot me." Kate snatched Holly's nail scissors from a pot on the shelf. She grabbed a hunk of hair. "I'm gonna cut it all off."

"Don't you dare," Holly said. "You can dye it brown, or—"

"No," Kate said. "No dye. Not touching that stuff again."

"It wasn't dye. It was bleach."

"Same difference."

"Then you'll have to wear a hat," Holly said. "Till it grows out."

Kate moaned. "Like, till for*ever*."

* * *

Kate used up most of the hot water. She stood beneath the shower and washed her horrible hair five times. But

47

it didn't make a lick of difference. Her hair was still a disaster, worse than a Halloween fright wig. Kate tied it all back with an elastic and slouched into the bedroom.

Holly had already gotten dressed—short-sleeved plaid shirt and a pair of faded jeans. She plucked a bandana off the dresser and knotted it around her neck. "Okay," she said. "What do you want to wear?"

Kate shrugged. "I don't care."

"Then let's play it safe," Holly said. She pulled Kate's white riding breeches and ratcatcher shirt off their hangers and tossed them on the bed. She rubbed a cloth over Kate's boots and smoothed wrinkles from her navy hunt jacket.

"This ought to do the trick," Holly said, as Kate climbed into her clothes. "And nobody will see your hair under this." She handed Kate her riding helmet.

Miserably, Kate crammed it on and tucked her hair inside.

"Perfect," Holly said. "Just don't take it off, okay?"

Already, Kate could feel an itch on top of her head. She gritted her teeth and ignored it. The day had barely begun, and she had a horrible feeling it was going to get worse.

5

A WINDING DIRT ROAD led to the big meadow, but Kate and Holly took a shortcut through the woods. Magician jogged most of the way, as if he knew something exciting was about to happen. Holly plodded along on Daisy, the good-natured pinto mare all the beginners rode. She'd wanted to ride Buccaneer, but Liz had vetoed it.

"Wow," Holly said, pointing. "Look at all that!"

Kate halted her impatient horse and stared at the familiar field. She'd jumped its hunt course a gazillion times on Buccaneer and Magician. She knew this field like the back of her hand, but she barely recognized it today.

Overnight, it had been transformed into a jungle of people and equipment. Film crews milled about, dodging

49

camera dollys, arc lamps, and cables. Technicians wearing earphones were setting up a loudspeaker system.

"Testing, testing," boomed a disembodied voice.

At the far end of the field stood a round white tent that looked as if it once belonged to a circus. It even had a flag on top. Kate half expected to see a couple of clowns come tumbling out.

A thought struck her.

Would she have to wear makeup? Would somebody want to style her hair? No way was she going to take her helmet off.

Giles Ballantine's assistant rushed up to them. In one hand he clutched an iPad; in the other he held a Starbucks cup that was dangerously close to spilling over. Magician snorted and danced sideways.

"Easy, boy," Kate said, patting his neck.

"I'm Tony Gibson," the assistant said. He took a sip of coffee, then glanced at Kate's white breeches, her highly polished boots. "Is this what you're wearing for the screen test?"

"It's okay, isn't it?"

"I guess so," Tony said. "I don't know much about riding clothes, but—" He shrugged. "Didn't the other girl tell you what to wear? Mr. Ballantine e-mailed her. She was supposed to forward it to you."

Mrs. Dean snagged his attention, and he turned away.

What was left of Kate's confidence collapsed. Who knew what Angela was wearing, but whatever it was, she'd conveniently forgotten to share the details. She was probably all decked out in a classical dressage outfit, complete with long-tailed coat, yellow vest, and a black top hat.

Suddenly, Magician jerked up his head and neighed. Mrs. Dean abandoned the director's assistant and fired up her video camera. She aimed it toward the woods.

"There's Angela," Holly said. "I bet she's been practicing on the cross-country course."

Kate scrunched up her eyes. She'd forgotten to bring her sunglasses. "What's Angela wearing?"

"Jeans and a pink t-shirt," Holly said. "And paddock boots."

"Oh, great," Kate muttered. "Just what I need."

Moments later, Angela trotted up.

"It's so hot," she said, looking directly at Kate. "Aren't you just *dying* in that jacket?"

Sweat trickled down Kate's neck. Her head itched in a dozen different places and she wanted to scratch them all. "I'm fine."

"Did you forget something, Angela?" Holly said.

"Like what?"

"An important e-mail?" Holly said. "From *Uncle* Giles?"

"Oh, that," Angela said. "I forwarded it, but Kate obviously ignored it." She gave a little laugh. "It doesn't matter, though. This screen test is mine."

"Of course it is, darling," said Mrs. Dean.

Angela smiled, then pulled off her helmet and shook out her hair. Black and shiny, the way it always was.

* * *

"I don't believe it," Holly said. "It was a *wig*, a stupid blond wig, and we all fell for it."

Kate nodded, too miserable to speak.

Bad enough she was wearing the wrong clothes, she'd just ruined her hair for no good reason. It would take a year to grow out. Everyone would laugh and make stupid jokes, and who knew what Liz would say. Kate clenched her fists. If she wasn't so desperate for her own horse, she'd ditch the screen test and go home— maybe even all the way back to Connecticut.

Just then, Liz drove up in the barn's truck. She parked beside the mobile canteen and got out, shot a quick glance at Angela and Mrs. Dean now talking to Giles Ballantine, and told Kate to switch tops with Holly.

Her plaid shirt would look more casual than Kate's formal white ratcatcher. They could change in the tent while Liz held their horses.

"That's better," she said, when the girls emerged. "Now, give me your jacket, Kate. And take off that helmet. You don't need it yet."

"Thanks, but I'm okay."

"Let's go sit in the shade," Holly said. "We can watch Angela make a fool of herself."

"She won't," Kate said, as they led their horses toward a stand of old trees. "But I will." She loosened Magician's girth and ran up her stirrups. "Correction. I already did."

Holding Magician's reins, Kate plonked herself down beneath a large maple. Its branches formed a leafy canopy over tussocks of switch grass and a formidable clump of thistles. From here, they had a full view of Angela jumping the hunt course. An enormous mobile camera, mounted on tracks, kept pace with her. So did Giles Ballantine riding a yellow golf cart. It was enough to spook the steadiest horse, but it didn't seem to faze Skywalker one bit.

Standing on the sidelines, Mrs. Dean filmed it all.

"Good thing you didn't bring Buccaneer," Holly said. "He'd have turned himself inside-out over this."

"Yeah," Kate said. "Even Magician's a bit spooky."

"Skywalker's going like a dream," Holly said, pulling Daisy away from the thistles. "But you guys will do better."

"Keep telling me that," Kate said.

Through his megaphone, Giles Ballantine barked out instructions, and Angela swung into a hand gallop. Up and down the meadow she went, crouched over Skywalker's neck like a steeplechase jockey. Now and then, she took a glance over one shoulder, as if someone were following her. It was a flawless performance—just what the script called for—until Mrs. Dean tripped over a cable and got yelled at by a sound technician.

"Serves her right," Holly said.

"She's worse than a soccer mom," Kate said, grinning.

Holly stiffened. "Uh-oh. We've got an audience."

"Where?"

"By the woods," Holly said, pointing. "It's probably that old guy who lives on the other side of the mountain. Mom said to keep away from him."

"Is he dangerous?"

"Nah, he's just a bit odd," Holly said. "He lives in a shack with goats and chickens and sells funny looking vegetables to summer visitors who are stupid enough to buy them."

Kate saw a brief movement, and whoever was there disappeared. Moments later, Giles Ballantine yelled, "Cut," and called for his crew to head into the woods. They'd do more filming in there, on the cross-country course. Mrs. Dean followed them, purse clutched in one hand, video camera in the other.

"Ouch," Holly said, scrambling to her feet.

"What?"

"These miserable prickers," Holly said. "They're all over me." She yanked off a clump of burrs and tossed it toward Kate. It missed and landed on Magician's saddle pad.

"Thanks a lot," Kate said.

"This stuff's worse than Velcro," Holly muttered.

Carefully, Kate picked off the burrs. One landed on her breeches and embedded its tiny barbs in her thigh. Magician tried to eat it.

"It's not food, you silly horse."

"I'm thirsty," Holly said. "I'm going to get a soda. Want one?"

Kate shook her head. "I'd only barf if up."

Holly led Daisy toward the mobile canteen, where

Robin, Sue, and Jennifer were tucking into doughnuts and orange juice. Kate yawned. She'd barely slept the night before. Did she have time for a short nap? She tightened her grip on Magician's reins, then settled back and closed her eyes. Just for a few minutes. That's all she needed.

* * *

As if from a great distance, she heard voices, someone shouting. Kate's eyes blinked open. Where was she? More important, where was Magician? In a panic, she looked around and saw him standing about twenty feet away, grazing. Somebody was holding him. One of the film crew? No, it was an old guy with a gray ponytail and overalls that looked as if they hadn't been washed in years.

"Your horse wandered off," he said, leading Magician toward her. "You shouldn't be sleeping when you got animals to take care of." He handed Kate the reins. His fingers were bony, like claws. There was enough dirt under his nails to grow potatoes.

"Thanks," she mumbled.

His mouth creased into a toothless grin. "Don't nobody thank me much nowadays." He pulled an odd-looking carrot from his pocket. It was shaped like a hand with three fingers and a thumb. "Okay if I give him this?"

Before Kate could reply, Magician snarfed it up.

"Good boy," the man said. Then he turned and shuffled off. Prickers clung to the back of his filthy overalls like barnacles on a rock.

Kate shuddered. He really was creepy.

He was also right. She shouldn't have fallen asleep. Feeling embarrassed and stupid, Kate looked around to see if anybody else had noticed, but there was no sign of Holly or the others. They were probably inside the tent.

Kate plucked another burr from Magician's saddle pad. She found two more tangled in his forelock and a couple down by his withers. They were multiplying like rabbits.

Angela trotted up. "They want you, like, right now."

"Where?"

"At the canteen," Angela said. "And you'd better hustle. Mr. Ballantine's waiting."

Kate started to tighten her girth.

"No time for that," Angela said. "Just run over there. Go on. I'll hold your horse." She leaned down and took Magician's reins from Kate's hands.

"Thanks." Kate hesitated. It wasn't like Angela to offer help, but if the director said he wanted her, she had better go.

"Ah, there you are," Mr. Ballantine said, when Kate ran up to him. He removed his sunglasses and smiled at her. His eyebrows seemed bushier than ever. "You saw what Angela did, right?"

"Yes."

"I want you to do exactly the same. We'll start off in this field. You can warm up over the easy fences, and after a couple of gallops, we'll go into the woods for more jumping."

Kate nodded. "Okay."

Whatever he wanted was fine with her. She just wanted to get it over and done with. Moments later, Holly and Daisy, followed by Liz and the rest of the riding team, joined them. So did Angela, leading Magician and Skywalker.

Kate released her chin strap and wiggled her helmet from side to side. Her head was so hot, you could fry an egg on it. She'd do the strap up again once she was on board.

"Here's your horse," Angela said. "His girth is loose."

Kate took the reins. She lifted her saddle flap and tightened the billets. One notch, then two. She tried for a third, but couldn't quite make it.

Magician squealed and pinned his ears.

That was odd. He'd never done that before. Maybe he was as nervous as she was. Kate stroked his neck, then stuck her foot in the stirrup and swung herself into the saddle.

In a flash, her world exploded.

Magician was everywhere at once. He bucked and reared, then bucked again. Up and down, snorting like a wild thing as if determined to get rid of his rider. Kate clung to his mane for dear life. Faces, jumps, and trees careered past in a blur. People scattered like chickens.

"Hit him between the ears," someone yelled.

"No," Liz shouted. "Pull his head away, Kate. Use your reins."

She tried, but it was too late. Magician was too strong. He plunged and twisted. He jackknifed into a bone-shattering buck, and Kate went flying off his back.

6

SHE CRASHED ONTO HER SIDe with a whump. Instinctively, she covered her head and rolled away from Magician's flying hooves. He let out another violent buck, then landed on all four feet and stood there, trembling and breathing hard as if waiting for some unknown demon to set him off again.

Arms reached out. "Are you all right?"

"Don't move her." That was Liz.

"Did you see it?" said a gruff voice. "Like, man, that horse was wild."

"Did anybody get this on film?"

Giles Ballantine elbowed his way through the crowd. "Should I call the medics?"

"I'm all right," Kate said. "I don't need help."

"Maybe you don't," Holly whispered, "but your hair does." She ripped off her bandana and covered Kate's shockingly yellow hair, now plastered to her sweaty scalp like wet straw.

Somewhere in all this mess, her helmet had gone missing.

"Where's Magician?" Kate said. She couldn't see beyond the forest of legs that surrounded her. "Is he okay?"

"He's fine," Holly said. "Jen's got him."

Liz knelt beside Kate and checked her for injuries. "Did you bang your head?"

"Just my arm," Kate said. It was only a little bit sore. Not enough to make a fuss about.

"Well, I guess that's it, then," Giles Ballantine said.

Kate rounded on him. "What do you mean?"

"You're hurt. You can't ride now."

"Oh, yes, I can," Kate said, through gritted teeth.

Holly took Magician's reins from Jennifer. The big horse looked nothing like the maniac that had erupted moments before. His ears were pricked, his eyes bright and inquisitive. He nudged Holly's pockets with his nose, obviously hoping for carrots.

So why had he freaked out?

Something she'd once read shot into Kate's mind. "When a perfectly well-behaved horse suddenly goes ballistic, there are two reasons—pain or fear."

Feeling a little dizzy, Kate stood up.

Magician was fine till she got on his back. So there had to be something wrong with his saddle. But what? It was the same one she always used. Kate laid one hand on the pommel, the other on the seat, and pressed. Magician shifted sideways. She pressed a little harder. He grunted and stamped his foot. Carefully, Kate released Magician's girth and pulled off his saddle. At first she didn't see them, but Holly did.

"Prickers," she said with a gasp.

They clung to Magician's withers the way they'd clung to the creepy guy's overalls. More were embedded in Magician's saddle pad. No wonder he'd flipped out. Gently, Kate removed them. Tiny barbs, sharper than fishing hooks, pricked her fingers and drew blood. She winced.

"You mean *that's* all it was?" said Giles Ballantine. "I thought horses were tougher than that."

"Their skin's more sensitive than ours," Liz said. She pulled a clump of burrs from Magician's saddle pad and tossed it to the director.

He caught it in one meaty hand.

"Now squeeze hard, then imagine you've got a hundred and fifty pounds of saddle and rider pressing on top of it."

He grimaced. "Okay, I get the picture."

Kate glanced at Angela. She was sitting on Skywalker with a guarded look on her face. Did she have anything to do with this? Prickers were insidious little beasts, but they didn't get underneath saddles without help.

"Okay, folks," Giles Ballantine said. "This is a wrap. Let's start packing up."

"A wrap?" Kate said. "What do you mean?"

"We're done," he said. "I'm sorry, but—"

"No," Kate said. "I'm going to ride."

"You can't," Liz said. "Look at Magician's back. It's rubbed raw, right where the saddle presses hardest. Put one on him now, and he'll go bananas."

"I know," Kate said. "I'm going to ride bareback."

Suddenly, Angela was there. "You *can't*," she sputtered. "You'll never get over those jumps in the woods without a saddle."

"I've been jumping bareback since I was five," Kate said.

Holly dusted off Kate's hat. "Then you'll need this."

Kate grabbed the helmet and crammed it down hard,

on top of Holly's spotted bandana. She tightened her chin strap, way past caring how she looked.

"Are you sure about this?" Liz said.

Kate's heart thumped a little faster. "Yes."

"Then don't take any chances, okay?"

"I won't," Kate said. "Can you give me a leg-up?"

Liz cupped her hands around Kate's knee and hoisted her on board. Magician trembled, just a little, but didn't squeal or kick out. Kate rubbed his neck and shoulders, then checked his sore spot. With luck, her thighs wouldn't rub against it.

"Promise you'll stop if it gets to be too much," Liz said. "I don't want you falling off again."

"Don't worry," Kate said. "I'll be careful."

"So will Magician," Holly said. "He knows what he's doing."

The director mounted his yellow golf cart. The camera crew and technicians took up their positions. Kate trotted toward them, but Angela got there first.

Her voice had an edge to it. "You can't do this."

"Do what?" Giles Ballantine said.

"You can't let Kate ride this scene bareback." Angela was almost screaming. "It's too dangerous. It's irresponsible. A good rider would never do such a thing. *I* certainly wouldn't try it."

64

"That's fine," the director said. "But if Kate's okay with it, then so am I."

Angela yanked Skywalker around till he was broadside to Magician. She grabbed Kate's reins. "You're a fool, Kate McGregor. You already fell off once, and you're gonna do it again."

"Nice try, Angela," Kate said. "Now let go of my bridle, and get out of my way."

"Then it's *your* funeral," Angela said, and rode off.

A camera trundled past, followed by yards of cable and two guys balancing a boom microphone. The director's assistant kept track of everything on his iPad.

Giles Ballantine looked at Kate. "Are you sure about this?"

"Yes."

"I don't want you taking any chances," he said.

"I'm ready," Kate said.

"Okay, then let's roll it," the director said. He barked a string of orders to his crew and told Kate to wait for his signal.

* * *

The clapperboard snapped shut and Kate was off. She leaned into Magician's flying mane and felt some of her old confidence return. It wasn't going to be easy without a saddle, but riding Magician bareback was a breeze. He didn't have sharp, knife-like withers like some horses did.

They cleared the brush jump, the crossrail, and the double oxer. Magician didn't seem to notice the mobile camera or the yellow golf cart that bounced along beside him like a rubber duck in a bathtub.

At the director's command, they galloped up and down the field, the way Angela and Skywalker had done. Kate glanced back over her shoulder. First left, then right. She tried to look as terrified as possible.

"Excellent job," Giles Ballantine boomed.

The unit manager called for a short break. One of the cameras needed adjustment, so Kate left the film crew and jogged back to the tent.

"Fantastic," said Robin.

Sue grinned. "You guys were awesome."

"Epic," said Jennifer. "You'll win, for sure."

Liz gave Kate a thumbs-up, then ushered her team inside the tent for an early lunch. Angela was over by the big maple, with Skywalker grazing among the pricker bushes. Only Holly remained, holding Daisy's reins and sitting on a metal folding chair. Beside her was a red cooler. She flipped it open, plucked out a bottle of water, and handed it to Kate.

"Thanks." Kate drank it thirstily.

"The prickers," Holly said. "I bet Angela—"

"Don't even go there," Kate said.

"Why not?"

"Because we can't prove anything," Kate said. "Those prickers are all over the place. You and I were chucking them about like beach balls. There's one in your hair." She leaned down and yanked it out.

Holly flinched. "I'm serious."

"So am I," Kate said. "But keep a lid on it, okay? Besides, it might've been somebody else." The thought had just struck her. *That creepy old guy*—maybe he put the prickers under her saddle.

"But why would he?" Holly said when Kate told her what happened. "He did you a favor by catching my horse."

"You said he was crazy."

"Not crazy. Just a little odd," Holly said.

"Whatever," Kate said. She glanced toward Angela. "Just make sure she doesn't follow me."

"Don't worry," Holly said. "I'll sit on her, if I have to."

Tony Gibson materialized beside Kate. "We're ready."

"Me, too." Kate gathered up her reins.

* * *

Kate wasn't sure what to expect. Giles Ballantine rattled on about "the big picture" and "lots of action." He waved his arms—wide, sweeping gestures—but was vague about the details. Just a few jumps, he said. Maybe the stream. They'd all have cameras. Another would follow her. She'd be captured on film from every possible angle. It all seemed a bit much, just for a stunt-double role, but Kate didn't care. As long as she won the part, they could film her upside down if they wanted.

Magician jumped the post-and-rails, with only a sideways glance at the camera mounted on a platform above it. Kate could hear the camera whirring as it cranked around to follow her down the path. Then came the log pile, and Magician didn't even falter as they soared over it.

So far, so good.

But, next up was the palisade—a solid board fence that spanned the width of the trail. On both sides, thorn bushes formed a dense barricade. Kate glanced up. One cameraman was perched in a tree, another was crouched on the ground waiting to film her from beneath.

Magician didn't even hesitate.

He soared over the fearsome looking jump like he'd

just sprouted wings. Kate let out a sigh of relief. The worst was over. The rest of the jumps were easy, including the stream that ran alongside the trail.

No problem. Magician wasn't scared of water.

But Giles Ballantine threw her a curve. "I don't want you to jump it or ride across it. I want you to gallop *down* it."

"You can't gallop in a stream," Kate said. "Too many rocks."

"Whatever," he said. "Just keep moving. I need lots of action. Make a big splash."

The stream was close to overflowing its banks. Kate had never seen it so full. Magician needed no urging. He loved water. He loved to lie down and roll in it. Happily, he plunged down the bank. Then stopped, water churning around his knees. His legs started to buckle.

"Don't even *think* about it," Kate said.

"Faster, faster," ordered the director. "Keep moving."

Kate tried her best. She used her legs, her voice. She begged and pleaded with Magician to move forward, but he ignored her. He began to paw. First one foot, then the other. He splashed about like a toddler till Kate was soaked to the skin.

It felt amazingly good.

"Enough," Kate said. She kicked him, hard. Harder than she ever had before.

But Magician had other ideas. His front legs folded like the spines of a broken umbrella. Down went his nose, followed by the rest of him. With a contented sigh, Magician collapsed into the water.

* * *

Holly couldn't stop laughing. "You let him *roll*?" she said over and over. "I can't believe it. You should've kept him moving. You know what he's like."

"I couldn't stop him," Kate said. "He's a bulldozer."

"More like a motorboat," Holly said, still laughing.

The film crew had laughed as well. They thought the whole thing was a huge joke. And, of course, they'd captured it all on video. Giles Ballantine said not to worry, that Kate had ridden well and he'd be making his decision in a couple of days. One of the cameramen told Kate that Angela and Skywalker had trotted down the stream without a problem.

Just my rotten luck, Kate thought, as she and Holly rode back to the barn. She'd survived the prickers and getting dumped, and she'd done everything else by the book, only to hit a brick wall because Magician was more sea horse than land horse.

"Stop worrying," Holly said. "Mr. Ballantine's got to choose you. You're much better than Angela, and besides," she added with a scowl, "none of us will be able to live with her if she gets the part."

"We won't be able to live with her if she *doesn't*," Kate said.

"Great," Holly said. "We lose either way, huh?"

7

HOLLY READ ADAM'S text message again. He hadn't used crazy shortcuts the way he usually did. He'd actually typed whole words that made sense. Holy hugged her cell phone and sighed. It was almost midnight, but no way could she go to sleep now.

"Don't tell me," Kate said. "Adam just texted?"

"How did you guess?"

"Because you've gone all goofy."

Under the bedside lamp, Kate's yellow hair glowed like a dandelion in full sun. It had already caused a minor sensation at the barn. Angela had scoffed, but the other girls loved it, especially Jen who changed her hair color every week.

"Funky," she'd said.

Liz had been diplomatic. "It'll grow out."

Holly gave another sigh. Kate's nose was firmly buried in the latest *Young Rider*. Holly had already skimmed it. It was full of the usual cool stuff, but nothing was as cool as the news Holly was dying to share. Finally, when it was obvious Kate wasn't going to ask, Holly blurted it out.

"Adam's gonna be in the movie," she said, barely able to contain her excitement. "Giles Ballantine's hired him as the stunt double for Nathan Crane."

Kate looked up. "Nathan Crane?"

"He's playing the part of Ian Hamilton," Holly said. "You know, the cute guy who keeps rescuing Ophelia Brown."

The news about Nathan Crane winning the plum *Moonlight* role had just exploded all over Facebook. The fan sites were going wild. Was he dating Tess O'Donnell? Would he get to kiss her in the last scene? But trust Kate to act dumb. She wouldn't recognize Nathan Crane if she fell over him, but she certainly knew his name.

"Can he ride?" Kate said.

Holly threw a pillow at her. "He'll be here on Monday."

"Who?"

"Adam, stupid. Who did you think?"

"Nathan Crane?" Kate said.

Holly rolled her eyes. "How I wish."

She'd told Kate a million times about Nathan Crane, but Kate never listened. If a guy didn't ride horses, he wasn't on her radar.

But Nathan Crane was definitely on Holly's radar.

He had streaky blond hair, quirky eyebrows, and a deep voice that made him sound older than seventeen. Would he actually come to the barn? Would Tess O'Donnell? Giles Ballantine hadn't said. They could do amazing stuff with computer graphics these days, so maybe the stars didn't need to be at every movie location in person.

Holly scrolled through Adam's message one last time.

He hadn't even tried out for the role. Giles Ballantine needed a guy who could ride like a maniac, and Adam volunteered. Even his horse, Domino, was a perfect fit. He was a flashy, black-and-white half-Arabian, just like the one Ian Hamilton rode in the book.

* * *

The following afternoon, Tony Gibson called Kate and told her to meet Mr. Ballantine in Liz's office. He'd be bringing Angela with him. They'd be there in ten minutes.

Ten minutes?

That was just enough time to sweep the aisle, or fill a few water buckets, or maybe tack up Magician and run away. Kate grabbed a broom. She absolutely *had* to keep busy.

"Chill out," Holly said. "It'll be over soon."

"Big help you are," Kate said, sweeping vigorously. "Don't you get it? He's bringing Angela with him."

"So?"

"It means *she's* got the part."

"No, it doesn't," Holly said. She took Kate's broom and hung it up. "It means he's just being polite, that's all. He's been staying with the Deans, remember?"

All the more reason to worry. Angela had probably wrapped *Uncle* Giles around her little finger by now. When required, she could lay on the charm thicker than the makeup she wore.

Wiping her hands on a cloth, Kate allowed Holly to drag her into Liz's cramped office. Kate wished she was here, but Liz had gone to a committee meeting with Mrs. Dean, which meant Angela's mother wouldn't be here either. Maybe that's what Mr. Ballantine wanted—no interference from parents. Not that Liz was Kate's parent, but she was close enough.

Kate checked her watch. "Two minutes."

"And counting," Holly said.

She parked herself in a nest of saddle pads on top of a tack trunk. Kate sat on a metal crate, then got up again. She shut Liz's rusty file drawer that refused to stay shut and poked her head into the aisle. Neat and clean, the way she'd left it. Even the rakes, brooms, and pitchforks were lined up precisely in their racks.

"Stop flitting about," Holly said. "You're driving me nuts." She scrunched over to make room on the tack trunk.

Kate flopped down beside her, feeling sick. Moments later, she felt even worse when the director showed up with Angela simpering beside him. She wore a pink t-shirt and black jeggings and a self-satisfied smile. Giles Ballantine had obviously told her she'd be getting the part. Kate could even imagine his first terrible words: "Kate, I'm so sorry, but—"

Liz's old swivel chair creaked as the big man settled himself into it. He cleared a space on the desk for his iPad. "Okay, girls. "Here's the story," he said. "You both rode fantastically well. Your horses were fabulous, and—"

Gloom settled over Kate like a wet blanket.

She heard the director's voice droning on about how amazing she and Angela were and how honored he was that they rode for him, and blah, blah, blah. But all Kate could see was Angela, preening in front of a camera and getting paid a thousand dollars, only to blow it on stupid stuff like designer shoes or another tennis racquet when she already owned a hundred.

Holly nudged her. "Pay attention."

"It wasn't an easy decision," the director said, swiping through screens on his iPad. "I had to run the film many times before I made up my mind."

Kate held her breath.

Giles Ballantine smiled at Angela, now leaning against the doorframe and examining her nail polish like it was the most important thing on her mind. "You were spectacular out there," he said, "and your Skywalker's a fine looking horse, but"—there was a dramatic pause— "I've decided to use Kate for the part."

"Oh." Kate's hand flew to her mouth.

Holly gave her a fist bump. "Epic!"

"But why?" Angela said. "Why Kate and not me?"

"Because Kate rode bareback," Giles Ballantine said. "It suits the scene better."

"What scene?" Angela snapped.

"When Ophelia's running away."

"But *she's* not riding *bareback*," Angela said. "I read the book, and—"

"So did I," Giles Ballantine said. "I read it several times. But when I saw Kate riding without a saddle, something clicked. I decided to change the story, and my scriptwriter agrees with me."

In two strides, Angela was at Liz's desk. She slammed down both fists. Pencils and paperclips went flying. Liz's old phone almost jumped off its hook. "If *I'd* ridden bareback," she said, looming over Giles Ballantine like a vulture, "would *I* have gotten the part?"

"Maybe," he replied. "But you said you'd never jump without a saddle. That it was irresponsible and—"

"I did not," Angela yelled. "I never said that."

Giles Ballantine tapped his iPad. "I'm afraid you did," he said. "My assistant keeps track of everything."

There was a stunned silence.

For a moment nobody moved. Even Holly was frozen to the tack trunk. Then Angela's breath came out in a whoosh. She tossed back her hair, shot Kate a look of pure hatred, and swept out the door.

"Well," the director said. "I'm sorry to disappoint her, but that's the way it goes in this business." He smiled at Kate. "You won't mind riding that scene again without a saddle, will you?"

Kate grinned. She'd ride it without a *bridle*, if he wanted.

"So, Kate McGregor," he said. "What do you say? Do you want the part, or not?"

* * *

To celebrate Kate's success, Liz whipped up a batch of peanut-butter cookies, which left the girls speechless because Liz never baked. Ever. They were even more speechless when Liz announced she was going on a cruise. An old friend from college had just won two last-minute tickets to the Bahamas and invited Liz to go with her. She would be gone for five days but back in time for Kate's filming.

"I've asked Bea Parker to come and help out," Liz said.

Holly cheered. "Yippee. I love Aunt Bea."

"Who's Aunt Bea?" said Kate.

"She's not really an aunt," Liz said. "Just an old friend of my mother's who taught me to ride. She used to breed and show Morgans, but now she writes mysteries and books for horse-crazy girls."

"Like us," Holly said, grinning.

While Liz went off to sort clothes and pack for her trip, Kate and Holly pored over the revised script Giles Ballantine had given them. There would be three scenes:

Scene 1: Ophelia's riding bareback in jeans and a t-shirt. She runs into a gang of motorcycle thugs, and they chase her through the woods. To shake them off, she gallops down narrow trails and over the palisade, but the motorcycles follow her.

"That's crazy," Kate said. "Motorcycles can't jump."

"I know," Holly said. "But it doesn't matter because this is fantasy, okay?"

Scene 2: The time portal. Ophelia veers off the trail and rides between two giant redwoods. Fade out. Cue special effects.

"Redwoods?" Kate said. "This is Vermont, not California. We don't have giant redwoods here."

"So what?" Holly said. "They'll just find a couple of pines and disguise them."

Kate grinned. "A tree makeover?"

Scene 3: Ophelia gallops out of the time portal dressed in a long, white gown. The motorcycle guys have morphed into zombies on horseback. They're about to grab Ophelia when Ian Hamilton rides to the rescue.

Holly sighed. "Angela's going to be *so* jealous over this."

"She already is," Kate said.

"And all because her stupid trick backfired," Holly said. "It got you the part instead of her."

"We don't know for sure that she did it."

"C'mon, Kate," Holly said. "Who else put those prickers under your saddle? The Tooth Fairy?"

Kate laughed, but underneath it all, she was worried. The filming wasn't for another week. That was plenty of time for Angela to cause even more trouble.

8

ARMED WITH A LAPTOP and five pounds of carrots for
Magician, Bea Parker arrived at noon the next day. She
was a tall, angular woman with mischievous brown eyes,
corkscrew curls the color of traffic cones, and a pair of
horn-rimmed glasses that dangled from a beaded chain
around her neck.

"Ms. Frizzle from *The Magic School Bus*," Kate
whispered.

Holly shook her head. "*Harriet the Spy*."

Aunt Bea laughed. She swept Holly into a bone-
crunching hug, shook hands with Kate, and shoved Liz
briskly out the front door with instructions to have fun.
"And if you don't have fun," she warned, as Liz climbed
into her car, "we won't let you back in the house."

Kate grinned. She had a feeling they were going to have a lot more fun than Liz.

"Okay, kids," Aunt Bea said. "Here's the deal. Tell me how much help you need around the barn, and I'll pitch in. I'm an absolute whiz with a pitchfork and broom. I'll even scrub muck buckets, but don't expect me to cook. I'm the only person alive who can burn water, so I'm counting on *you* to feed me."

Holly eyed the laptop. "Are you writing a new book?"

"You bet," Aunt Bea said. "And this afternoon I'm going to shut myself in your mother's bedroom and try to figure a way to rescue my hapless hero from a gang of horse thieves."

"*Horse* thieves?" Kate said. "Like, for real?"

"Yes," Aunt Bea said. "I thought they died out with the buggy whip manufacturers, but apparently not." She hefted her laptop onto the kitchen table and fired it up. "Three valuable horses were stolen from a show barn in Maine last month. I heard about it on the Web, and it gave me the idea for my latest novel."

"Did they find the horses?" Holly's eyes were wide.

"Let me find out," Aunt Bea said, scrolling through multiple sites. "I guess not. The police are still working on it, like I am with my new book." She closed her laptop. "So don't interrupt me unless you have a crisis, okay?"

"Don't worry," Holly said. "We've already had our crisis ration for the week."

Aunt Bea raised her eyebrows. "Anything I could use for fodder?"

"Fodder?" Kate said.

"For my stories."

One by one, Holly rattled off Angela's nasty tricks, and by the time she was through, Aunt Bea's eyes were shining. "You've just given me an idea for a whole new kids' series," she said. "I'm going to call it *Barn Bratz*."

* * *

Later that afternoon, Kate was schooling Buccaneer in the outside ring when Giles Ballantine drove up. He'd exchanged Mrs. Dean's silver Mercedes for a white convertible with steer horns bolted to its front bumper. The rear doors swung open and Angela stepped out, followed by a girl wearing cargo pants, purple clogs, and a black baseball hat. The director gave them a cheery wave, then roared off in a cloud of dust and exhaust fumes.

Kate shaded her eyes. The sun was behind Angela and her friend, so it was kind of hard to see them. But the girl looked vaguely familiar. Kate was sure she'd seen her before, but where? A horse show? The local Starbucks? Curious, Kate rode a little closer. The girl pulled off her baseball hat and masses of blond hair tumbled out.

It was the girl in Holly's magazine.

Angela had her by the arm. She was dragging Holly's favorite star toward the barn, and poor Holly was in the wash-bay scrubbing grass stains off Daisy's legs. By now, she'd be soaking wet. She'd be covered with horse hair and soap scum, and Angela would lead Tess O'Donnell right by her on the way to Skywalker's stall.

Unless Kate got there first.

She surprised Buccaneer with a swift kick, and he bolted forward. They zoomed out of the ring, shot past Angela and Tess, and skidded into the barn.

Kate jumped off her horse and shoved him in his stall, then sprinted along the aisle. The wash-bay was halfway down, and there was Holly, looking even worse than Kate imagined—a poster girl for bedraggled barn rats.

"Quick, hide," Kate gasped, breathing hard.

Holly looked up. "Why? What's wrong?"

"She's coming."

"Who?"

"Tess O'Donnell," Kate blurted. "Mr. Ballantine just dropped her off with Angela. They'll be here in, like, two seconds."

Holly's mouth fell open. She whipped around, still clutching the garden hose. It squirmed and spat like a snake, spraying water all over the barn.

"Turn it off," Kate yelled.

But Holly wasn't fast enough. She fumbled with the nozzle and twisted it in the wrong direction. Jets of cold water pulsed out. They thundered into stall doors, bounced off the cement floor, and clobbered Angela and Tess O'Donnell like pellets from a paintball gun.

In a flash, Kate cranked off the tap.

"You idiot," Angela screamed. "Look what you've done." She flapped her hands as water dripped down her face. It looked as if she'd just walked through a fountain. Her flimsy sundress was plastered to her legs like wet newspaper.

"I'm sorry," Holly said, turning red.

Tess O'Donnell grinned at her. "It actually felt pretty good. I was kinda hot, anyway." She shook out her hair, then stuck her baseball hat back on. It had *Moonlight* embroidered across the front in neon pink letters that matched her tank top.

"I really am sorry," Holly said. "I didn't mean to—"

"No big deal," the star said. She thrust her hand toward Holly. "I'm Tess O'Donnell."

"I know," Holly said. "And I'm Holly the klutz."

Tess laughed.

Kate said, "I'll get you a towel."

"Get a dozen," Angela snapped. "And hurry up."

* * *

Kate zoomed into the tack room and rounded up all the towels she could find. They were threadbare and ripped, but reasonably clean. She raced back and gave the nicest one to Tess. Angela grabbed the others. There was no sign of Holly or Daisy—just a puddle of dirty water and an empty halter dangling from the cross-ties.

Kate suddenly remembered Buccaneer.

"I'll be right back," she said. "Gotta untack my horse."

Tess followed, wiping off her arms. They were tanned and muscular, with a tiny rose tattoo on her right shoulder. She looked through the stall bars as Kate removed Buccaneer's saddle and bridle. Their workout was so brief that he hadn't even begun to sweat and didn't need cooling out.

"What's his name?" Tess said.

"Buccaneer," Kate said. "And he loves Life Savers."

"Me, too."

"Want to give him one?" Kate pulled a roll from her pocket.

There was a moment's hesitation, and Kate saw the same worried expression on Tess's face that she'd seen in that magazine photo. Buccaneer stamped his hoof, impatient for treats.

Tess backed away. "Are you riding him in my scenes?"

"No," Kate said. She fed Buccaneer a handful of mints. "I'll be riding Magician, Holly's horse. He's out in the paddock. Want to go and see him?"

"Is he anything like this one?"

"No," Kate said. "He's a lot gentler. You'll love him."

"I'm gonna have to," Tess said, sounding doubtful. "Giles wants me to get used to him, for close-ups and stuff. He told me to ask you for advice."

"No problem," Kate said. "I'd love to help."

"That would be great."

Angela strolled up. "I'm sure Kate's much too busy, with the movie and everything," she said. "So why don't I teach you?"

Tess shrugged. "Well, okay, I guess."

"Fabulous," Angela said. "And we'll start right now, with *my* horse." She balled up her wet towels and dropped them on the floor. "Then we'll hang out with Uncle Giles and my parents at the club. Do you play tennis?"

Tess glanced at her cargo pants. "Yes, but I'm not—"

"No problem," Angela said. "Mother just bought me a really cool new tennis dress. It'll fit you perfectly." She linked arms with Tess and shot Kate a feral smile, then ushered the star toward Skywalker's stall with the expertise of a tour guide.

Why hadn't Giles Ballantine warned them about Tess?

Not that Kate really cared, one way or another. But Holly did. For her, meeting Tess O'Donnell was a big deal. It would be like Kate meeting Ineke Van Klees or Nicole Hoffman—women most people never heard of unless they devoured *Dressage Today* or *Young Rider* the way Kate did.

Tess was kind of cool, though. She hadn't batted an eyelid over being drenched with the garden hose or minded drying herself off with a ratty old beach towel.

The door banged open, and Holly slouched into the

barn. A clump of Daisy's white hair clung to her shoulder like a pet mouse. Her face was blotchy, and it looked as if she'd been crying.

"Hey, are you all right?" Kate said.

Holly sniffed and wiped her nose. "I'm just peachy."

"It was a dumb accident," Kate said. "But it was worth it, just to see Angela's face."

"Yeah, but now Tess thinks I'm a total spaz."

"She doesn't." Kate gathered up Buccaneer's saddle and bridle. "Wanna go home for a swim?"

"Sure," Holly said. "Then I can drown myself."

"Idiot," Kate said. "Wait here while I put Buccaneer's stuff away." She gave Holly the rest of her Life Savers. "Spoil him for me, okay?"

Holly stuffed half of them in her mouth.

The tack room was across the aisle from Skywalker's stall. Angela was inside, smothering her horse with fake kisses, while Tess kept her distance in the aisle. Kate wiped off Buccaneer's bit and hung up his bridle, then hoisted her saddle onto its tree. She was about to leave when Angela's voice stopped her cold.

"Poor Kate McGregor," Angela said. "I feel so sorry for her."

"Why?" Tess said.

"Because Kate's mom is dead and her father's abandoned her," Angela went on. "She's working here and living with the Chapmans because she's got nowhere else to go."

Kate almost choked. Didn't Angela know she was in the tack room? Or was she doing this on purpose, knowing Kate would overhear? Heart thumping, she peered through a crack in the wall. She could see both girls quite clearly.

"That's awful," Tess said. "Poor Kate."

Angela gave a dramatic sigh. "That's why I told Uncle Giles to give Kate the part. He really wanted me to do it because I'm a much better rider than she is, but Kate needs the money, desperately."

"You're very generous."

"It's the least I could do," Angela said.

Tess nodded. "Kate's lucky to have you for a friend."

* * *

Kate was trapped. She couldn't leave the tack room till they'd gone or Angela would know she'd overheard them. Finally, they wandered off, talking about Angela's new tennis outfit, and Kate burst out of her hiding place and into Buccaneer's stall. Holly was feeding him the last of the mints.

"Did you hear that?" Kate cried.

"What?"

"Angela, spewing lies again."

Holly sighed. "What is it this time?"

Kate spat out the words, but all Holly did was shrug. She was obviously feeling too sorry for herself over the garden hose incident to feel much sympathy for anyone else.

"Ignore her," Holly said. "Nobody will believe her, anyway."

"Tess will," Kate said. "Angela's really got her claws into her. She's going to teach her to ride."

"That's a joke," Holly said. "Angela couldn't teach a cowboy to ride a rocking horse." She crumpled the empty mint packet and stuffed it into her pocket. "Did Mr. Ballantine ask her to do this?"

"No," Kate said. "According to Tess he wants *me* to teach her, but Angela butted in and took over."

"Hah," Holly said. "Let's see how long *that* lasts."

* * *

It lasted all of two hours. Giles Ballantine called when Kate and Holly were back at the barn, turning Magician and the ponies outside for the night.

"How'd you get on with my lovely star?" he boomed.

"Fine," Kate said, as she unclipped Magician's lead rope.

Had the director heard about Tess's unexpected shower? Had Tess complained about it? She didn't seem too bothered at the time, but maybe Angela had persuaded her that Kate and Holly weren't to be trusted.

"We're going to shoot a few scenes tomorrow morning," the director went on.

"Tomorrow?" Kate said. "But it's Saturday."

He laughed. "Makes no difference to a movie crew."

"What sort of scenes?"

"Close-ups of Tess and Magician." There was a pause. "I'd like you to work with her before we start shooting. She's a little nervous around horses."

"I know." Kate hesitated. "But Angela's going to help her."

She heard traffic noises, followed by a police siren. Giles Ballantine was probably on the highway in his fancy white convertible and about to get a speeding ticket. The siren wailed past, then faded.

"I want *you* to do it," he said. "You're the stunt double for this movie, not Angela."

"But—"

"Don't you want to?"

Of course she wanted to. Not for herself, but for

Holly. She was the one who loved all this stuff—the glitter and the makeup, the fan magazines. Lots of horsy girls did, including Jennifer and Sue. They were beyond excited about the movie deal. Angela was, too, even though she pretended not to care.

"Yes," Kate said. "Of course, I do."

"Then just do it," he said, and hung up.

* * *

By dinner time, Holly had gotten over being embarrassed about drenching Tess O'Donnell with the hose and saw the funny side of it. Over macaroni and cheese from a box, she regaled Aunt Bea with every last detail until they were howling with laughter.

"More fodder?" Kate said.

Aunt Bea wiped her eyes. "Definitely. This stuff just gets better and better." Her smile faded. "Unlike my wretched book. I have to drive into Boston on Monday. Will you guys be okay on your own for a day?"

"Is anything wrong?" Holly said.

"No," Aunt Bea said, sighing. "Just more research I didn't expect."

"Can't you e-mail or Skype?"

"Not this time," Aunt Bea said. "The guy I'm interviewing is in jail."

"Yikes," Holly said. "What did he do? Steal a barn full of horses?"

"Not quite," Aunt Bea said. "He's a crooked race-track lawyer, and he's got a lot of insider stories." She picked up a pencil and stuck it behind one ear. "So, will anything important be happening while I'm gone?"

"Adam's coming," Holly said.

Kate winked at Aunt Bea. "Holly's boyfriend."

"He's not," Holly said, turning bright pink.

"Yeah, right," Kate said. "You only spend half the day on the phone with him, and the other half waiting for him to call."

"Tell me about Adam," Aunt Bea said.

While Holly launched into stories about Adam and Domino and their roles in the film, Kate slipped into the bedroom she shared with Holly. She needed time alone to think about what Angela had told Tess.

Most of it was true.

Tears sprang to Kate's eyes. She could still see her mother, packing school lunches, meeting her off the bus, and reading with her at night. Horse books, always horse books. Mom had ridden as a kid, growing up in England, and she wanted the same for Kate. So, despite her father's indifference, Kate had taken riding lessons. Mom was always there—at the horse shows and clinics—telling Kate that winning wasn't important, but having fun and feeling good about yourself was.

It all ended five years ago when Kate was nine.

One day Mom was there; the next day she wasn't.

Dad said it was a heart attack. Then he'd gone very quiet and shut himself away from Kate. She kept her mom's memory alive by riding the best she could and not allowing creeps like Angela Dean to get the better of her.

Kate gulped and dried her eyes.

She loved her dad. He was an absent-minded professor who preferred critters with fuzzy legs, compound eyes, and four wings to real people. He hadn't exactly abandoned Kate, but he wouldn't win any prizes for keeping in touch. He was in the Amazon, chasing butterflies, and Kate had no idea when he'd be back.

Angela had even told the truth about Kate living with the Chapmans because she had nowhere else to go. Well, except for Aunt Marion's tiny house in the village. But that wasn't an option any more because Aunt Marion had gone on vacation.

The latest issue of *Seventeen* lay on Holly's bed.

Kate glanced at Tess's photo.

How was she supposed to work with Tess O'Donnell and gain her respect if the actress thought she was some penniless kid Giles Ballantine had taken pity on?

THE BARN WAS ALIVE with film crew by the time Kate and Holly arrived at seven the next morning. They fed the horses and mucked stalls and were just finishing up when a large motor home trundled down the driveway. It had *Giles Ballantine Productions* in gold letters along both sides.

"The star's dressing room," Holly said.

Kate leaned on her broom. "How do you know?"

"Stars always have mobile dressing rooms on location," Holly said. "Tess needs a place to change and rest up between scenes."

"What's wrong with our tack room?" Kate said.

Holly sighed. "She can't change in *there*."

"Why not?" Kate said. "We do it all the time."

Just then, Giles Ballantine drove up in his white convertible. He barked out a string of instructions, and the film crew leaped into action. They moved cameras, adjusted arc lamps, and laid more cables. Tony Gibson told Kate she had an hour to help Tess prepare.

After that, Tess would be in makeup and wardrobe.

She jumped out of the motor home wearing faded jeans and a red t-shirt with two penguins on the front. Her blond ponytail stuck out the back of her black baseball hat. From this distance, she looked like Holly.

* * *

Kate scanned the director's notes. He would be shooting two scenes. One camera would film Tess leading Magician out of the barn; another would capture her in close-up, getting on him.

"Without a saddle?" Tess said.

Kate nodded. "Yeah."

Tess looked up at the rafters, as if hoping to see a giant hook that would hoist her on board. So far, she'd managed to swallow her fear and feed Magician a couple of carrots. She'd also led him up and down the aisle, and she even laughed at one of Holly's lame jokes.

"Show me," she said.

In one fluid movement, Kate vaulted on Magician's back.

"You're dreaming," Tess said. "I'll never be able to do that."

"You will," Kate said. "It's really easy."

Kate knew she was lying, but she had to be upbeat for Tess's sake. In truth, vaulting took lots of practice, and it suddenly dawned on Kate that she'd made Tess's job a whole lot tougher by riding the scene bareback. If she hadn't, Angela would've won the stunt-double role, and Tess would be riding Skywalker with a saddle instead of Magician without one.

"Have you done any gymnastics?" Holly said.

Tess shrugged. "I'm pretty good on the balance beam and kind of okay with the pommel horse."

"Perfect," Kate said, sliding off Magician. "Wanna try him?"

"Okay," Tess said. "But how?"

"I'll give you a leg-up." Kate took off her helmet and gave it to Tess. "But put this on first."

"Why?"

"Barn rules," Kate said. "Nobody rides without one."

Tess swapped her baseball hat for the helmet, then

raised her left knee so Kate could lift her onto Magician's back. She was light as a feather, thank goodness. It would make vaulting much easier for her.

"Good," Kate said. "Now get off him, like I did."

Tess leaned forward, swung her right leg over Magician's back, and landed on the ground with a soft thud. Her knees buckled, and she staggered against Magician's shoulder.

"Whoops," she said. "Was that okay?"

"You're doing great," Holly said.

Kate gave Tess another leg-up, and Holly kept Magician busy with carrots as they practiced over and over. After ten minutes, Kate announced that Tess was ready to vault.

She *had* to be ready. They didn't have a choice.

The director was waiting, along with a film crew that cost hundreds of dollars per minute. He'd made it quite clear that he expected them to be ready on time and that Tess would be able to vault onto Magician's back like an expert.

"Must I?" Tess said, looking doubtful.

Kate nodded. "It's in the script."

"It wasn't in the first one."

"I know, and I'm sorry," Kate blurted. "It's my fault.

You'd be riding with a saddle if I hadn't ridden bareback, but—"

"It's okay," Tess said. She sucked in her breath. "Giles is right. This makes the scene much more powerful, so let's do it."

As they led Magician outside, Kate's admiration for Tess grew. Holly's favorite star buckled down and got on with her job. In half an hour, she'd have to vault onto a horse that scared her death in front of cameras and a bunch of people who'd be filming her every move.

"Pretend he's a pommel horse," Holly said, "in the gym."

"Okay, but where are the handles?" Tess said.

"His mane will have to do." Kate grabbed a handful and demonstrated the vault again.

It took her six tries, but Tess finally got it. She landed on Magician's back and just sat there, wide-eyed and gaping like a goldfish, as if she could hardly believe where she was.

"Awesome," Holly said. "That was amazing."

"Nice," Kate said, grinning. "Now get off and do it again."

"Slave driver," Tess said. She gave them a cautious smile, then slid to the ground, gathered up a hunk of mane, and hoisted herself back onto Magician as if she'd been doing it forever.

Kate heaved a sigh of relief. They'd pulled it off. She hadn't thought they would, but they'd taught Tess to vault with five minutes to spare. The film crew cheered. They'd been hanging out at the mobile canteen, drinking coffee and eating doughnuts and waiting for this moment.

Still smiling, Tess leaned forward and wrapped her arms around Magician's neck. "I think I love this horse."

"We all do," Holly said, proudly. "He's the best."

Kate saw a flicker of movement. It was Angela, sliding out of the barn. She looked both ways, as if worried someone had seen her, then pasted a fake smile on her face and strolled toward them. Giles Ballantine fell into step behind her. He walked up to Tess and patted her knee.

"Well done," he said. "That's just want I wanted."

"Thanks." Tess gave him a happy grin. "I couldn't have done it without Kate. She's an amazing teacher."

"She's a great little rider, too," Giles Ballantine said. "She has lots of guts, which is why I chose her."

Angela made a noise in her throat. Her smile slipped a few notches and disappeared completely when Tess slid off Magician and surprised Kate with a fierce hug that almost knocked the breath out of her.

"Oh, boy," Holly whispered. "You're in for it now."

"Why?"

"Duh-uhh," Holly said. "Look at Angela's face. She thinks you've just stolen her new best friend."

Kate was about to argue when Tony Gibson ran up.

"We need Tess in makeup and wardrobe," he said, tapping his watch. "Like, right now."

Smoothly, Tess linked her arm through Angela's. "Come with me," she said. "You can help choose my outfit. You're *so* good at that sort of stuff, and I'm hopeless. I can never get it right."

Angela shot Kate a look of pure triumph.

"Wow," Holly said, once the girls were out of earshot. "That was really smooth." She nudged Kate. "Tess has done you a huge favor, really huge."

"What?" Kate said.

Holly rolled her eyes. "She's just declawed Angela."

* * *

The other riding team members arrived, all excited about watching Tess's scene. Sue and Robin dragged two sawhorses outside to sit on; Jennifer settled for an upturned muck bucket. Aunt Bea showed up, wearing denim overalls and a floppy straw hat. From a large, quilted bag, she pulled juice boxes and granola bars and handed them out, then parked herself in a metal folding chair that Kate found in Liz's office.

Kate and Holly ran back into the barn.

Holly groomed Magician again, even though he was already polished to perfection, while Kate headed for the tack room. They'd been using a halter and lead rope for Tess to practice with, but now Magician needed his bridle. Holly had cleaned it earlier, and there it was, on the wooden peg beneath her saddle, except its cheek pieces were empty.

So, where was Magician's bit?

It had to be here, somewhere. Kate checked Holly's grooming box. She rummaged through the tack trunk they shared, then pulled it away from the wall in case Magician's bit had fallen behind. There was no sign of his thick rubber snaffle.

Holly stuck her head around the door. "What's keeping you?"

"This." Kate held up the bridle. "Where's his bit?"

"I left it on my peg," Holly said. "I was going to attach it, but then Mr. Ballantine and Tess arrived, and—"

"Well, it's not there now," Kate said.

"That's impossible," Holly said. "It can't just disappear."

The door banged open and Aunt Bea strode into the tack room. "What's disappeared?"

"Magician's bit," Holly said. "We can't find it."

Aunt Bea waved toward a large metal hook filled with bridles and bits of all shapes and sizes. "Then use another one."

"We can't," Kate said. "Magician's bit is a rubber snaffle. He won't go in anything else." It was extra thick, and there wasn't another like it in the entire barn.

Kate checked her watch.

Five minutes till Tess got out of makeup and wardrobe, which left them no time to rush down to the village tack shop for a replacement. Not that they'd have one in stock—rubber snaffles like Magician's had to be special ordered.

Okay, so where did that leave them?

Without the bit, Tess would have to use Magician's halter, which was no big deal, given that she already had during practice. But that meant Kate would have to use it as well. This scene demanded continuity. If Tess rode with a halter, so would Kate. Trouble was, she'd be galloping over fences and fleeing motorcycles with nothing more than a lead rope. Maybe her silly thought about riding the scene without a bridle was about to happen— for real.

Kate tried not to panic.

The film crew's clock was ticking. Giles Ballantine wouldn't take kindly to a delay, which meant that Angela could easily persuade him to switch gears and have Tess vault onto Skywalker instead of Magician. And then Angela would get to ride the rest of the scene, just the way she wanted.

Aunt Bea's voice brought Kate back to earth.

"No problem," she said. "Kate, find me some vet wrap. And Holly, see if you can dig up a spare D-ring snaffle or an eggbutt, okay? I'll need scissors, as well."

Within minutes, Aunt Bea solved the problem.

She wrapped the soft, spongy bandage around an ordinary snaffle and declared that Magician wouldn't know the difference. And he didn't. Mouthing his new bit, he walked out of the barn with Tess by his side and stood perfectly still while she vaulted on his back. The cameras captured it all, including Tess's black wig that made her look exactly like Ophelia Brown.

Kate couldn't take her eyes off it.

Then someone handed Tess a riding helmet. She crammed it on over her wig, and the camera zoomed in for a close-up. Angela gushed about Tess's performance as if she'd masterminded the whole thing herself, but

Kate felt nothing but stupid. She wanted to cover her ugly, bleached hair with a brown paper bag, jump into a hole, and slam it shut behind her.

"Be cool about it," Holly said. "Pretend you don't care."

Angela sniggered as she sauntered past them, arm-in-arm with the star. "Tess is signing autographs in the village this afternoon," she said. "And I'm going with her."

"Good for you," Holly muttered.

Kate glared at Angela's smug expression. Had *she* stolen Magician's bit? If so, when? Kate's brain cycled backward. They'd worked with Tess and Magician in the barn, then come outside to practice vaulting, which left Angela free to slip inside the tack room and steal the very thing Magician needed most.

But there was no point in challenging her—not in front of Tess and the film crew. Besides, Kate had no proof. But she'd find it, somehow. She'd track down that missing bit, and then she'd confront Angela with it.

10

ON MONDAY MORNING, Holly leaped out of bed talking a mile a minute because Adam was coming. She ransacked her closet, emptied drawers, and changed her mind half a dozen times before settling on denim jodhpurs, a lime green tank top over a white t-shirt, and her brown paddock boots with rainbow laces.

Casual, but not too casual, she told Kate. She didn't want Adam to think she didn't care, but she didn't want him to think she did, either. By the time Holly left to feed the horses, their room looked as if it had been blasted by two hurricanes at once.

Kate flopped back onto her pillow.

What a luxury, sleeping in for once. She forgot about Holly's fashion dilemma, snuggled beneath her covers, and was about to doze off when Holly burst back into their bedroom.

"Magician," she shrieked. "He's gone."

"What?" Kate rubbed her eyes.

Holly grabbed her by the shoulders. "He's not in the paddock. Come on, get dressed. You've got to help me find him."

Still half asleep, Kate pulled on her breeches, struggled into a gray hoodie that was inside-out, and followed Holly to the barn. Last night, she'd fed the horses and turned Magician out in the back paddock. Then she'd secured the gate with a metal chain because Magician was a wizard at opening the latch. So if he got out, it meant one of two things: Either he'd jumped out or someone had let him out.

He could be miles away by now.

The woods, trails, and meadows around Timber Ridge Mountain covered five hundred acres, most of which Holly and Kate hadn't even explored. There was plenty of room for a horse to get lost.

"We'd better tell Aunt Bea," Kate said. "She'll know what to do."

"She's gone to Boston, remember?" Holly said. "She left before I got up. She's got an interview with some prisoner guy about her new book, the one with the—"

"Horse thieves?" Kate said.

For a moment, they stared at one another.

Holly's eyes widened. "You mean he could've been *stolen*?"

"No," Kate said, pulling herself together. She pointed to the gate. It was exactly the way she'd left it. "A thief wouldn't have chained the gate up again. He'd have left it wide open."

"I'm going to call Mom."

"She's on a boat," Kate said. "They won't have cell service in the middle of the ocean."

"Then I'll call the police." Holly whipped out her phone.

"Not yet," Kate said. "Let's try looking for him first."

* * *

Kate organized a search party. Robin and Sue would scope out the neighborhood, while Kate scoured the woods and trails with Jennifer. They'd keep in touch via phone whenever possible, but cell coverage on the mountain was spotty at best.

"What about me?" Holly said.

Kate tightened Buccaneer's girth. "Somebody's got to

stay here in case Magician comes back on his own," she said. "Besides, haven't you forgotten something?"

"What?"

"Adam's coming."

"Oh." Holly's hand flew to her mouth.

The barn door slid open and Angela sauntered inside. For an awful, suspicious moment, Kate wondered if *she* had anything to do with Magician's sudden disappearance. But that was ridiculous. Angela might've stolen Magician's bit, but even she wasn't stupid or mean enough to steal him as well.

"Where are you going?" Angela said.

"Magician's lost," Jennifer said, trying to calm her horse. Nostrils flaring, Rebel was ready to go. His bright chestnut coat gleamed like a newly minted penny.

"You lost a horse?" Angela said. "How careless."

"He jumped out of the paddock," Kate said, as she led Buccaneer from his stall. He pinned his ears, the way he always did whenever he was within ten feet of Angela. Kate felt like pinning her own ears as well. She'd like nothing better than to block out the sound of Angela's snotty voice.

Robin said, "We're going to look for him."

"And we could use your help," Sue added.

"Oh, I'm so sorry," Angela drawled. She flicked a wisp of hay off her immaculate white shirt. "But they're filming a scene in the village, and I promised Tess I'd go and watch. She'll be seriously bummed if I don't show up."

"So what are you doing *here*?" Kate said.

Angela ignored her and turned to Holly. "What will you do if you can't find Magician?" she said. "Are you going to tell Mr. Ballantine he's gone?"

"No," Holly said. "But I'm sure you'll do it for us."

Angela smirked. She pushed past Kate and flounced off.

* * *

Holly kept herself busy, mucking stalls and cleaning tack—anything to take her mind off Magician. She fussed with her hair and smeared on more lip gloss, as if that mattered at this point. Every time one of the horses whinnied, she raced outside in case it was Magician.

Or Adam.

He was supposed to be here by ten. It was now eleven-thirty. She'd texted him about Magician, but he hadn't responded. Holly leaned against the barn door and waited. Her cell phone remained stubbornly silent. No word from Adam. Not a peep from Kate or any of the others out searching for Magician.

Was he okay? Did he know the way home, or was he utterly lost? Was he stranded on a busy road with cars honking at him? Holly shrank into herself. If only Adam was here to keep her company, to help her stop thinking of all the awful things that could happen to her horse.

Finally, at noon, a red-and-black truck pulled into the driveway. Behind it was a matching horse trailer. Holly forced herself to stay calm, never mind that her heart was doing flip-flops. She and Adam had talked and texted every day, but they hadn't seen one another since a party at the Timber Ridge clubhouse when Holly was still in her wheelchair.

Adam had never seen her walk, let alone ride.

He climbed out of the cab and ambled toward her, looking kind of shy. "Hey," he said, dumping his knapsack on the ground. "How you doing?"

All Holly's carefully rehearsed words went out the window. "Magician's gone," she blurted.

"Gone?" Adam said. "Like where?"

"He jumped out of the paddock last night."

Adam glanced at the five-foot fence and whistled. "Some jump."

"Don't joke," Holly said. "I'm serious."

"Okay," Adam said, holding up his hands. "Tell me what happened."

It all came out in a rush. "We don't know if he jumped out or if someone stole him, because Aunt Bea says there are horse thieves around, except she's gone to Boston. And now everyone's out looking for him but I can't go because someone has to stay here in case he comes back and—"

"Slow down," Adam said.

Holly took a deep breath. This wasn't the way she'd imagined things. She'd dreamed of running toward Adam in a field full of daisies. She'd be wearing a floaty white dress, not grubby jodhpurs and a stupid green tank top that made her look like Kermit the Frog.

"But what if we can't find him?" she wailed.

"You will," Adam said. He punched her gently on the shoulder. "And I'll help, so let's get saddled up. You can ride Daisy, right?"

"Yes," Holly said. "But someone's got to be here, in case—"

"My buddy can stay." Adam waved toward the truck.

The driver's door opened, and a tall kid got out. He wore cutoffs and a black t-shirt with *Moonlight* written across the front in bright pink letters. He had streaky blond hair, just like Adam.

Holly blinked. Her eyes were playing tricks.

That wasn't really Nathan Crane who'd just gotten out of Adam's truck, was it?

* * *

Kate rode beside Jennifer through the woods. Overhead, giant oak, maple, and pine trees formed a dense canopy that turned the trail into a green, leafy tunnel. Now and then, shafts of sunlight broke through like spotlights at a theater. Whenever a side trail came up, one of the girls would trot down it, calling out for Magician, then circle back to the main one.

"No luck," Kate said, after her fourth detour. "He hasn't been this way." There was no sign of fresh hoofprints or manure on the ground.

"Do you think we'll find him?" Jennifer said.

Rebel's ears were pricked forward; his long mane flowed in ripples down his shoulders like a copper-colored wave. He jiggled his bit and danced sideways, anxious to run.

Kate gritted her teeth. "We've *got* to find him."

She couldn't begin to imagine Holly's heartbreak if they didn't. There were no grownups around to help, either—just a bunch of kids and an impatient film director who wouldn't care if a horse was missing. He'd just order up another one.

115

To keep her mind off Magician, Kate asked Jennifer about Beaumont Park, her grandmother's riding school in England. Caroline West was a former Olympic rider, and she'd invited Kate and Holly to train at the park next summer.

"Gran's got a full brother to Rebel," Jennifer said. "His name is Renegade, and I'm going to ride him when we go over there."

"Does he eat vanilla pudding as well?" Kate said.

Jennifer shook her head. "Renegade's a health nut. He prefers low-fat yogurt."

Kate laughed, then tried her cell phone again. Still no service. Her stomach rumbled, reminding her she'd forgotten to eat breakfast. The way things were going, she wouldn't get lunch either.

They were only a ten-minute ride from the barn.

"I'm going back to see if there's any news," Kate said. She'd also get something to eat. There were some leftover granola bars and juice boxes in the tack room. "Wanna come with me?"

Jennifer shook her head. "I'll ride out to the campground. Maybe one of the Boy Scouts has seen Magician."

"Perhaps they'll help us look," Kate said. "You know, for a badge or something."

"I'll ask," Jennifer said, and rode off.

* * *

There was no sign of Holly when Kate reached the barn—just the red truck and trailer that belonged to Adam's mother. There was no sign of Adam and Domino, either.

Kate loosened Buccaneer's girth, gave him a short drink of water, and left him in his stall. The one beside it was Daisy's, but it was empty, which meant only one thing—Holly had gotten fed up with hanging out at the barn and gone looking for Magician.

Adam had probably gone with her.

Feeling hungry enough to eat a saddle, Kate made for the tack room. Yesterday, she and Holly had torn it apart trying to find Magician's bit. They'd rummaged through tack trunks, upended all the grooming boxes, and climbed a stepladder to reach the highest shelves, but they hadn't found the rubber snaffle. Kate grabbed one of Aunt Bea's granola bars and opened up a juice box.

There was a noise behind her.

She whirled around, granola bar halfway to her mouth, and found herself face-to-face with a boy wearing earbuds and snapping his fingers to music so loud even Kate could hear it thumping. He pushed a hunk of streaky blond hair off his forehead and yanked out his earbuds.

"Hi," he said, grinning.

Kate took a step back, tripped over a curry comb, and collapsed onto a heap of saddle pads and horse blankets. Grape juice splattered all over her breeches and gray hoodie.

The boy held out his hand. "Sorry."

"Who are you?" Kate said, staring at his *Moonlight* t-shirt. They'd been appearing all over the village ever since the movie deal was announced. Almost everyone was wearing them.

"Tom Smith," he replied. "I'm a friend of Adam's."

"Are you working on the film?"

"Not really," he said, helping Kate her feet. "I'm just hanging out. What's your name?"

"Kate." She swallowed the last bite of granola and opened another juice. Apple, this time. Less messy. Tom took one for himself. He stabbed at his box with the straw and made a hash of it. Kate did it for him.

"Thanks," he said. "I never did get the hang of these things."

He was cute, really cute, with green eyes and long lashes that most girls would kill for. Kate suddenly wished she wasn't wearing her rattiest breeches and an inside-out hoodie that had grape juice all over it.

* * *

Tom said Adam had asked him to hang around the barn in case there was news of Magician, but he couldn't stay any longer. He had to return the truck and trailer to Adam's mother by three o'clock, and she lived fifty miles away.

"I'll come back in my car and get Adam," he said, hefting a duffle bag out of the truck. "Around five, or so. Do you think he'll be back by then?"

Kate shrugged. "I guess."

Tom climbed into the truck, rolled down the window, and stuck his head out. Kate, already mounted on Buccaneer, towered over him. She had a bird's eye view of the top of his head. There was a faint line of brown roots on either side of his part.

A guy who colored his hair?

He shot her a lopsided grin, then slapped the side of the truck with his arm, revved the engine, and drove off. As he disappeared around the corner, Kate thought about his hair. For some odd reason, it made her feel less stupid about her own.

11

HOLLY COULDN'T BELIEVE Kate hadn't recognized him. "You idiot," she said, pulling off Daisy's saddle. "That was Nathan Crane. *The* Nathan Crane. You know, the guy who—"

Kate shrugged. "He said his name was Tom Smith."

"It is," Adam said, "but the studio changed it. They figured *Nathan Crane* would make the girls swoon, and I guess they were right."

Holly threw a hoof pick at him.

She was a muddle of emotions. Half of her was terrified they wouldn't find Magician; the other half was over the moon about being with Adam and meeting Nathan Crane. He'd gone to grade school with Adam before his family moved to Hollywood and he became a teenage movie star. Adam, being a typical guy, hadn't warned her about this ahead of time. He didn't think it was important.

Kate removed Daisy's bridle and wiped off the bit.

"What did you think of him?" Holly whispered. She glanced at Adam. He was brushing Domino in the next stall and listening to his iPod. He couldn't possibly hear them.

"Who, Adam?" Kate said.

"No, silly, Nathan."

"Tom," Kate insisted. "Tom Smith."

"Whatever," Holly said. They'd had this conversation before, with Kate playing dumber than dumb, which meant she probably liked him. Holly was about to ask her again, when Aunt Bea strode into the barn, followed by Nathan Crane.

"This young man says we've got a missing horse," Aunt Bea said, glaring at Holly and Kate. "So you'd better tell me what's been going on, and then I'll bawl you out for not telling me sooner."

"But you were in Boston," Kate said.

"In a prison," added Holly.

Adam's eyebrows shot up. He looked at Aunt Bea, then at Nathan. "This sounds like it's gonna be really good," he said. "So let's stick around."

* * *

Aunt Bea took charge of the missing-horse operation with the efficiency of a drill sergeant. She sent Adam and Nathan off to the village for ice cream and two large pizzas, told Holly to gather up all the local maps she could find, and had Kate call the local Pony Club and 4-H leaders to ask for volunteers.

"Tell them to be here by nine tomorrow," Aunt Bea said.

In short order, she phoned the police, alerted the fire department, and convinced Mrs. Dean to e-mail the Timber Ridge residents and warn them to be on the lookout for Magician.

"He wasn't stolen," she announced over dinner.

Nathan took another slice of pizza. "How do you know?"

"Two things," Aunt Bea said. "First of all, thieves wouldn't have shut the gate behind them."

"Yeah," Adam said. "Who ever heard of a tidy thief?"

"And second," Aunt Bea went on, "they'd have stolen *all* the valuable horses—Buccaneer, Skywalker, and Rebel—not just Magician."

"Which means he jumped out," Holly said.

"Or someone let him out and closed the gate after him," Aunt Bea said. "But who on earth would do that?" She looked at each of the kids in turn.

Adam shrugged. "I dunno."

"Me neither," Nathan said.

Holly opened her mouth, but Kate nudged her sharply under the table, and Holly faked a sneeze instead. They had absolutely no proof—none at all—not even a tiny shred of evidence that Angela had taken Magician's rubber snaffle or let him out of the paddock.

All they had were suspicions.

* * *

Holly was curious. She wanted to know why Nathan had lied to Kate about his name. Well, not really lied. He just hadn't told the truth, which wasn't quite the same thing. While Aunt Bea was regaling Kate and Nathan with details of her latest book, Holly cornered Adam in the kitchen.

"Why did Nathan pretend to be someone else?"

"He didn't," Adam said. "He was just being himself. Plain old Tom Smith. He doesn't get to do that very often. Most girls throw themselves at him because he's Nathan Crane, the movie star, so meeting a girl who didn't recognize him was a surprise."

"Or a major disappointment," Holly said.

"Think about it," Adam said. "How would you feel if people only adored you because you were a teen idol?"

"I'd love it," Holly said, almost meaning it.

"You wouldn't," Adam said. "Trust me. Nathan's cool with his fans because he has to be, but he hates all the fuss and publicity. The paparazzi never leave him alone. They ask the dumbest questions, then ignore his answers and print a load of lies."

"Like he's engaged to Tess O'Donnell?"

Adam grinned. "And eats chocolate covered ants for lunch."

"Ugh." Holly shuddered. "Has he met Angela yet?"

"No," Adam said.

"I bet she'll throw herself at him."

"The way you did?"

"Did not," Holly said, indignantly.

"Yeah, right," Adam said. "Be honest. You'd have fallen over if I hadn't held you up."

"In case you've forgotten, Adam Randolph," Holly said, trying not to grin, "I've only just learned to walk again."

"And you do it really well," Adam said.

He leaned forward, and Holly thought he was going to kiss her, but Aunt Bea came into the kitchen, followed by Kate and Nathan. Adam reversed direction and punched her shoulder instead.

"Hey, dude," Nathan said. "You about ready to leave?"

* * *

Just before nine the next morning, Giles Ballantine drove up with his assistant. Had they come to help with the search? For a few crazy moments, Kate had visions of the movie director on his yellow golf cart, bouncing along the trails, with Tony Gibson beside him taking notes on his iPad.

The riding ring was filled with volunteers, warming up their horses and eager to get going. Aunt Bea handed out maps and carrots, coordinated cell phone numbers, and made sure someone in each group carried a halter and lead rope in case they found Magician.

"I'm sorry about your horse," the director told Kate and Holly. "And I know you're worried, but this gives me quite a problem as well."

Kate bit her lip. She knew what he was going to say.

"I'm willing to push the shooting back another day," Giles Ballantine went on. "But if your horse doesn't turn up by tomorrow night, I'll have to use Angela and Skywalker instead."

"But you can't," Holly burst out. "You've already shot two scenes with Magician and Tess."

"Then I'll just reshoot them with Angela's horse," he said. His voice softened. "Look, I'm sorry, but my crew is already working overtime to make the schedule, and I can't delay it any longer."

Five minutes after he left, Angela strolled into the barn. Wearing her best, wrap-around smile, she leaned against Domino's stall door and watched Adam saddling him up.

"He's so cool," she purred. "He matches the book exactly. I mean, Ian Hamilton's horse is a black-and-white half-Arabian, and so is Domino. He's perfect for the role, so totally perfect. Aren't you excited about it?"

Adam grunted and picked out Domino's left rear hoof. He set it down and picked out the other, seemingly oblivious to Angela and her inane remarks.

"What's *she* doing here?" Holly said.

"Volunteering?" Kate said.

Holly snorted. "When's the last time Angela volunteered for anything that involved work?"

From Buccaneer's stall, Kate could see Angela chatting to Adam, who was doing his best to ignore her. Had she somehow found out that Nathan Crane was here? Well, it wouldn't do her any good. Nathan was keeping a low profile. Aunt Bea had ordered him to stay inside the house until everyone left.

"If you show your face at the barn," she'd warned, "you'll cause a riot. We'll have girls swooning and falling off horses all over the place."

Kate finished tacking up Buccaneer. She led him out of his stall, past Angela, who was still trying to get Adam's attention, and into the riding ring. Aunt Bea had organized the volunteers into groups of three or four riders, but Kate decided to head out by herself. Buccaneer was faster than most of the other horses, and she'd be able to cover more ground on her own. Aunt Bea gave her a map and a handful of carrots.

"Good luck," she said, patting Buccaneer's rump.

* * *

After an hour of searching on familiar trails, Kate checked her map. Aunt Bea had assigned each group its own territory so they wouldn't overlap and duplicate their efforts. Part of Kate's designated region covered the other side of Timber Ridge Mountain. She'd never explored it before.

Ahead of her, was a three-way fork. Kate hung a sharp left and found herself on a wide-open ski trail. Every few hundred yards, other trails branched off through the woods. They had big metal signs with black diamonds and scary names like *Bear Trap*, *Jaws of Death*, and *Devil's Leap*. Buccaneer eyed them warily as if they were about to jump out and bite him.

Kate patted his neck. "They won't hurt you."

But he refused to be convinced. Skittering along the trail, he snorted at stumps, danced sideways around rocks, and almost turned himself inside out when a squirrel darted across the path.

The trail forked again.

This time, Kate went right and followed a much narrower trail that curved around the mountain, away from the ski area. The scenery changed. The woods became denser, the trail harder to follow. It twisted and turned until Kate had no clue what direction she was riding in. It was noon. She'd been gone almost three hours with no sign of Magician.

Time to start heading back.

She decided to take a different route and was about to turn around when she noticed hoofprints. They were faint and scattered, but definitely there. She bent down and looked closer.

Did they belong to Magician?

Trying not to get her hopes up, Kate followed the prints, up one trail and down another. Trouble was, these hoofprints could belong to anyone. Lots of riders came this way. She checked her map again and realized she'd ridden right off it.

She needed to ask for directions, but where?

Ahead of her was a small, tumbledown house. It was little more than a shack with peeling paint, broken windows, and a tin roof that looked ready to collapse. Wisps of smoke curled from a rusty pipe, so the place wasn't deserted. Kate rode closer. Maybe whoever lived here had seen Magician or could tell her how to get home. She was about to call out when the front door banged open and a man lurched down the front steps.

He had a gray ponytail, bare feet, and filthy overalls. In one hand, he clutched a bottle; in the other, he held a shotgun. It was aimed directly at Kate.

She froze, unable to move.

This was a dream, a very bad dream. In a moment she'd wake up and find herself laughing about it with Holly. But the man was real and so was his gun. He took a step toward her.

Kate zapped herself into action. She slammed both heels into Buccaneer and he bolted down the trail like a barrel racer. They careened around the next corner and galloped another two hundred yards before slowing to a trot. Buccaneer was breathing hard. So was Kate. That man was the same creepy guy who'd caught Magician when she fell asleep at her screen test.

Was there some sort of connection here?

All of a sudden, the trail ended. A huge pine had fallen across the path and blocked it. Kate looked for an escape route that didn't involve going back past the old man's house.

On her left were dense trees, giant boulders, and thorny bushes—impossible to get through. To the right was a rickety wooden fence topped with barbed wire. Beyond it was a scrubby field full of junk cars, old tires, and garbage bags spewing rubbish. A half dozen chickens scratched in the dirt. An emaciated goat grazed beside an old bathtub filled with scummy green water. Off to one side stood a wooden shed in worse shape than the man's house. A strong gust of wind would probably send it flying.

Buccaneer pricked his ears and whinnied.

Was he calling for another horse?

Kate stood up in her stirrups and looked in all directions. There was no sign of a horse—just the goat and the chickens. Disappointed, she sank back into her saddle but kept a close eye on the shed. Buccaneer was still staring at it, ears on full alert, like he knew something was in there.

He whinnied again, and a scruffy brown mare limped out.

She had overgrown hooves, a tangled mane that fell to her shoulders, and watchful eyes set far apart in a finely boned head. Kate guessed she was a chestnut, but it was impossible to tell beneath all the grime. Twigs, mud, and burrs had turned her coat into camouflage. It looked as if she hadn't been brushed in years.

Kate slid off Buccaneer's back and tied him to a tree. She pulled two carrots from her pocket. The mare hesitated, like she didn't know what to do. She sniffed the carrots, warily, then lipped them up. Kate caught a glimpse of her teeth—a young horse, probably no more than five or six years old.

Flies swarmed around the mare's delicate ears. Kate brushed them off and was so busy examining the rest of her that she failed to notice another horse coming out of the shed. It wasn't till she got nudged, firmly, that she looked up.

"Magician!" Kate shrieked.

He whickered and leaned across the fence.

Kate flung her arms around him. She buried her face in his mane. "I don't believe it," she said, close to tears. "I've found you." She reached for her cell phone to call Holly, but there was no service.

Stupid cell towers. Never there when you need them.

Kate pocketed her useless phone. She ran her hands over Magician's neck, down his shoulders, and along his withers, looking for signs of injury. Apart from being covered in dust, he seemed fine. He nuzzled the brown mare, and she nuzzled him back. They looked kind of sweet together. Kate shared the last carrot between them.

"I've got to get you out of here," she said.

But there was only one gate, and it led from the field into the creepy guy's back yard. No way was she going to use that.

The wooden fence wasn't very high. No more than four feet, and there was a narrow section that didn't have barbed wire on it. Kate took the halter off Buccaneer, buckled it onto Magician, and attached the lead rope. Then, without hesitating, she climbed over the fence, vaulted onto Magician's back, and trotted around piles of trash to the center of the field. She grabbed hold of Magician's mane.

"Okay, boy," she said. "Let's go."

Magician bounded forward. In three strides he cleared the fence and landed safely on the other side. Kate jumped off his back, untied Buccaneer, and swung herself into his saddle.

The brown mare gave a soft, pitiful whinney.

It broke Kate's heart to leave her behind, but she had to get out, and get out fast, before the creepy old guy realized what she'd done. Leading Magician, she rode past the old man's house, trying to be as quiet as possible.

Buccaneer had other ideas.

He let out an ear-piercing neigh. Hooves clattering on the gravel, he snorted and danced sideways, then shied at the tree stump he'd passed without a second glance just a few minutes before.

"You *idiot*," Kate said. "It's not gonna hurt you."

Magician nipped at Buccaneer's neck, as if ordering him to get a move on. Buccaneer squealed and pinned his ears. He whirled around, and Kate almost fell off, trying to control him while not letting go of Magician. She had to keep them both moving forward, but Buccaneer dug his toes in like a fractious toddler and refused to budge. In desperation, Kate slapped his shoulder with the lead rope.

In a flash, it was gone, ripped from her grasp.

12

BONY FINGERS CLUTCHED Magician's lead rope. "This is *my* horse," the man hollered. "Now get out of here before I call the cops."

"No," Kate screamed. "He's mine."

She kicked Buccaneer, hard. The big horse swung sideways and knocked the old man off balance, but he clung onto Magician like a limpet. At least he didn't have his gun. Kate kicked Buccaneer again. He let fly with a magnificent buck that whumped the old man's backside and sent him sprawling in the dirt.

Kate seized her chance.

She grabbed Magician's lead rope. Buccaneer, now raring to go, rocketed out of the danger zone with Magician beside him, matching him stride for stride. It was

almost like riding two horses at once, and for an exhila-
rating moment, Kate forgot to be scared. Pumped up
with adrenaline, she leaned into Buccaneer's flying mane.

"Go, go, go," she yelled.

Around the next corner they zoomed, and Kate
didn't slow down till they reached a fork in the trail.
Heart thumping like sneakers in a dryer, she fumbled for
her map. She had no idea where they were.

But the map wasn't in her pocket.

She whipped out her cell phone. Still no service. She
punched in Aunt Bea's number, just to be sure, but the
phone remained stubbornly dead. Okay, now what?

Jungle telegraph? Smoke signals?

She'd been lost in the woods once before, and Magician had brought her safely home. Maybe he could do it
again. Kate slid off Buccaneer, swapped his reins for the
lead rope, and vaulted onto Magician's back. Then, she
gave him his head and crossed her fingers he'd choose
the right path.

* * *

Ever since she met Adam, Holly had dreamed of something like this—riding through the woods with an awesomely cute guy who liked horses as much as she did.
Except this wasn't a dream. It was rapidly turning into a

nightmare. Adam tried to keep her mind off it with jokes and silly stories.

"What do you call a horse wearing Venetian blinds?"

"I dunno," Holly said.

"A zebra." Adam tapped his lips. "Okay, how about this one? When do vampires like horse racing?"

Holly shrugged.

"When it's neck and neck," Adam said.

She knew he was only trying to help, but it wasn't working. Her anxiety level had already gone into orbit. It was now three o'clock, and there was no sign of Magician—not even hoofprints or black tail hairs snagged on a thorn bush. She dialed Aunt Bea's number. The signal was weak. Holly could barely hear her.

"No news," Aunt Bea said. "Except Angela's still here."

"Doing what?"

"Throwing herself at your movie star."

"Poor Nathan," Holly said, not feeling sorry for him at all. It was Kate she felt sorry for. She'd finally met a guy she liked—even if she wouldn't admit it—and Angela was all over him. Then again, so were a gazillion other girls. Kate didn't stand much of a chance.

"I imagine he's used to it," Aunt Bea said. "Now, tell me—"

The phone cut out. Holly shook it and hit redial, but they'd ridden out of range. "Let's go home," she said. "I'm wiped out."

"Maybe someone else has found him," Adam said.

Holly gave him a weak smile. "Maybe."

It took them two hours. Except for Kate, they were the last ones back. The Pony Club volunteers had already checked in and left. Robin, Sue, and Jennifer were cooling off their sweaty horses; Aunt Bea was helping two 4-H kids load their ponies onto a trailer. She closed the ramp and walked up to Adam and Holly.

"Has Kate called?" Holly said. She got off Daisy's back, and her legs folded like spaghetti. This was her longest ride since before the car accident.

Aunt Bea hoisted her upright. "Not yet."

"Where's Nathan?"

"He left an hour ago," Aunt Bea said. "Giles Ballantine whisked him and Angela off to a barbecue. We're supposed to join them."

"I don't feel like celebrating," Holly said.

Aunt Bea took Daisy's reins. "Me neither."

Just then, Domino let out a loud neigh. Nostrils flaring, he skittered in circles around Adam and almost knocked him over. Daisy's ears perked up. She gave a soft, welcoming whinney.

"Look," Adam said, pointing. "Over there."

Aunt Bea let out a whoop. "It's Kate," she cried. "And she's riding Magician."

* * *

Holly's eyes sparkled. Her smile was so big, it almost jumped off her face. She couldn't stop hugging Magician. She ran her hands all over him, the way Kate had done. Adam finally gave her a leg-up onto Magician's back because she was close to collapse.

Feeling close to collapse herself, Kate leaned against Buccaneer. She'd ridden hard, all the way home, convinced the old man would chase her. But he hadn't. Magician hadn't put a foot wrong, either. He'd lived up to his magical name by picking the right trail.

"Where did you find him?" Aunt Bea said.

Kate told her about the old man, his gun, and the other horse and how the only way to get Magician out of the field was to jump the fence.

"It's kind of weird he didn't jump out on his own," Adam said.

"Yeah," Holly said. "He could've escaped, easy-peasy."

"I don't think he wanted to," Kate said.

Holly stared at her. "Why not?"

"The brown mare," Kate said. "He was hanging about because of her. You should've seen the way he was nuzzling her face."

Daisy sidled closer to Magician. She nipped at his mane.

"Then you'd better not tell Daisy," Adam said, laughing. "I think she's got a crush on him."

* * *

After walking out their horses, they led them into the barn. Kate stared around in surprise. They'd had no time for chores that morning, yet everything smelled fresh and clean. The brooms and shovels were neatly lined up, and the wheelbarrows were empty. Even the aisle was free of hay and shavings.

"I mucked all the stalls," Aunt Bea said. "With Nathan's help. He's pretty handy with a pitchfork."

Adam groaned. "That'll ruin his image, for sure."

Kate wanted to ask where he was but was too embarrassed. Feeling herself blush, she led Buccaneer into his stall, took off his bridle, and fed him a couple of mints. Horses were a whole lot easier to deal with than boys.

They didn't pretend to be something they weren't.

* * *

Holly changed her mind about the barbecue. All of a sudden, she wanted to go. She wanted to share her good news with everyone, but most of all, she wanted to see Angela's face when she discovered Magician was back home, safe and sound.

"I still think she did it," Holly said.

Kate shook her head. "He jumped out."

"But he's never jumped out before," Holly said. "Never."

"Well, he did this time."

"I don't think so," said Aunt Bea from the doorway. "May I come in?"

Holly cleared a space for her on Kate's bed. It was less messy than her own, which was buried beneath tangled sheets and discarded clothes. After changing her mind a dozen times, she'd settled on denim cut-offs and a purple tank top decorated with stars and a glittery slogan that said, *I love my horse*.

"Tell me more about the old man," Aunt Bea said. "Have you seen him before?"

"Yes," Holly said. "He was hanging about at the screen test."

"He gave Magician a really weird carrot," Kate said.

"Like this one?" Aunt Bea pulled something orange

from her pocket. It had two fat roots, numerous bumps, and creepy looking hairs.

"Yes," Kate said. "Exactly like that one."

"Where did you find it?" Holly said.

Aunt Bea held up her hand. "Let's back up a minute. We've all been thinking that Magician either jumped out or was let out of the paddock, right?"

Kate nodded.

"And that the old man found him wandering in the woods."

"Yes," Holly said. "But—"

"Well," Aunt Bea said. "I did a bit of poking around while you kids were in the shower. You know, looking for evidence. It's what I do for a living, for my books and stuff." Her voice dropped to a stealthy whisper. "And I found this carrot."

"Where?" Kate said.

"On the ground, just inside the paddock gate."

For a moment, there was a shocked silence. Holly looked at Kate, then at the deformed carrot in Aunt Bea's hand. Mom had warned them about the old man. He grew odd-looking vegetables and posted photos of them on Facebook and Pinterest. One of his parsnips was a dead ringer for Abraham Lincoln.

"Nobody else grows carrots like that around here," she said, "which means the old man dropped it when he stole my horse."

"And closed the gate behind him," Kate said.

"Looks like it," Aunt Bea said.

Holly clenched her fists. "He's horrible," she said. "I hate him. He's a criminal."

"No," said Aunt Bea. "He's crazy. If he was a real thief, he'd have stolen all the horses, remember?" She dug out her cell phone. "This guy needs professional help. He isn't fit to be living alone."

"What about his horse?" Kate said.

"She'll probably go to a horse rescue center."

"Can we help?" Holly said.

Aunt Bea shook her head. "It'll be a legal matter, so it's best to let the authorities handle it."

"Like who?" Kate said.

"Animal welfare," Aunt Bea said. "But I'll start with the local police. The chief's a fan of my books." She punched in a number, explained the situation, and hung up. "Now, I don't know about you guys, but I'm starving. I could eat a—"

"Horse?" Holly said, with a shudder.

She glanced at Kate's horrified expression. They both

knew what would happen if the old man's mare wound up at the auction instead of a rescue farm.

* * *

Kate saw Nathan the moment they arrived at the barbecue. Dressed in chinos and a white polo shirt that set off his tan, he was sitting on the Deans' patio beneath a red umbrella with Giles Ballantine, Tess, and Angela. Her parents and Tony Gibson were at the next table.

Nathan gave Kate a cautious wave and tried to stand up, but Angela pulled him down again. He switched on his movie star smile.

"She's really got her claws into him," Holly whispered. "Just like with Tess O'Donnell."

Kate shrugged.

"Don't you care?" Holly said.

"No. I mean *yes*. I don't know," Kate said.

Her heart skipped a beat. It sped up and slowed down the way it did in front of cross-country jumps that looked way too big to get over. She felt herself blush. Maybe it'd be easier if she just grabbed a hamburger from the grill and went home.

Angela's laughter drifted toward them.

"She won't be laughing in a minute," Holly said.

"I'm going to tell Mr. Ballantine he's got his star horse back." She marched over to his table, dragging a reluctant Kate with her.

Giles Ballantine lumbered to his feet and almost bumped his head on the umbrella. "Hi, there."

"We found my horse," Holly said.

"Is he all right?"

"He's perfect," Holly said. "Couldn't be better."

"Excellent news," the director said. "Excellent." He stepped out from the shade and wagged his finger like a fourth-grade teacher. "Now, listen up everyone. The horse is okay, so we're good to go tomorrow morning."

Nathan gave Holly a high-five. "That is *so* cool."

Amid cheers from the film crew, Tony Gibson waved his iPad, and Tess shot Kate a dazzling smile. She was probably relieved she wouldn't have to ride the scene again on Skywalker.

Mrs. Dean frowned. She laid a well-manicured hand on Giles Ballantine's arm. "Does this mean my daughter won't be in the movie?"

"I'm sorry, but yes," the director said.

He didn't look the least bit sorry. He looked every bit as relieved as Tess. Kate glanced at Angela. Her face had paled beneath its tan. She opened her mouth, then closed it again, and Kate was suddenly glad that Angela wasn't responsible for Magician's disappearance.

For a second or two, they stared at one another.

There was a brief, awkward connection as if they were two outsiders who'd worn the same wrong outfit on the first day at a new school. Angela gave an imperceptible nod. She tossed her hair back over her shoulders, and the moment was gone. She whispered something in Nathan's ear. He laughed and gave Kate a sideways look.

She turned away.

No point in hanging around. Nathan Crane was definitely too busy for the likes of her.

13

Kate left the party at nine. She felt like a fifth wheel—Holly and Adam were holding hands beneath the table, and Angela had dragged Nathan inside to show off her house.

"She'll be giving him the grand tour," Aunt Bea said, walking home beside Kate. "I bet Mrs. Dean had her maid polish Angela's trophies, just to impress him."

"Whatever," Kate said. She kicked at a loose rock.

Aunt Bea said, "You like him, don't you."

It wasn't a question. Kate shrugged.

"And I think he likes you," Aunt Bea said.

But Kate didn't believe her. Nathan lived in a different world, a world full of glamorous people with tons of money and fancy cars, the same way Angela did. Her parents even had their own airplane and a beach house in Barbados. Angela knew how to talk to guys like Nathan Crane. Kate didn't. She only knew how to talk to guys like Tom Smith.

* * *

Liz called at eight-thirty the next morning. Her boat had docked in Miami, and she wanted to know what was going on. Holly filled her in as best she could, then put Aunt Bea on the phone to convince her frantic mother that everyone really was okay.

"Poor Liz," Aunt Bea said, hanging up. "She's just had five days in a tropical paradise, and now she's coming back to a madhouse."

The mobile canteen trundled past.

Holly grinned and skipped out of its way. She loved all the chaos, the absolute thrill of making a movie, and didn't want to miss a single second of it. Sue and Robin had volunteered to muck stalls and Jennifer had fed the horses, which left Holly free to hang out with Kate. Adam would be along at any minute. He'd just texted to tell her that Mrs. Dean had more or less kidnapped Nathan and Tess.

For a playdate with Angela? Holly texted back.

Two huge motorcycles roared up. Both riders wore

red bandanas, steampunk goggles, and black leather vests with dozens of silver studs. Tattoos covered their muscular arms from wrist to shoulder. One guy was as bald as an egg; the other had long hair and a beard that was even bushier than Giles Ballantine's.

"The real deal," Kate whispered.

Holly rolled her eyes. "Scary."

The men rode their bikes into the ring, engines on low throttle. Kate followed with Magician at a safe distance, but he didn't seem the least bit fazed by the noise and confusion. Holly was so proud of her horse.

Giles Ballantine said, "I'm glad you found him. I didn't want to have to reshoot Tess's scene with Angela's horse. I like this one much better."

"So do I," Holly said.

He beckoned Kate over and explained the sequence of shooting. The first scene would be Kate riding Magician through the woods where she runs into the motorcycle guys, who chase her over the cross-country course.

"All of it?" Holly said.

"It'll only look that way," Giles Ballantine said.

Special effects would be involved, he explained. For the most part, they'd be shooting Kate and Magician separately from the motorcycle riders. Later, they'd splice them together during the film editing process.

"So they really won't be chasing me, then," Kate said.

"Only over one of the jumps," Giles Ballantine said. "I want a wide-angle shot of you in front and the bikers behind, and we can't achieve that with camera tricks alone. You'll have to jump the palisade together."

"But how will the bikes get over it?" Holly said.

"They'll use a ramp."

"But that's not—" Kate sputtered. "That's not *real*."

Giles Ballantine roared with laughter. "Nothing about filming is real. Especially this one. It's a fantasy."

"What about the scene with the zombies?" Holly said. "After Ophelia rides through the time portal?" Nobody had mentioned this before.

"We're doing that one with computer animation."

"And Adam?" Kate said.

"He'll be riding to the rescue, as planned," Giles Ballantine said. "We'll be shooting that scene tonight, after it gets dark."

* * *

At noon, Giles Ballantine declared they were ready to begin rehearsals in the meadow. They did a couple of runs over the hunt course. Magician flicked his ears once or twice, then ignored the noisy motorcycles that roared along behind him. Kate even remembered to look scared and glance back over her shoulder.

"Good girl," Giles Ballantine said. "That's what I want."

This was no different from the audition—the same cameras and equipment, the same crew bustling about—except Angela wasn't there. Neither was Nathan Crane. Two days ago he was nothing more than a teen star in Holly's favorite fan magazine. Now, he was—well, Kate wasn't too sure what he was.

Angela's new boyfriend, perhaps?

After a short break, Kate rehearsed her rescue scene with Adam. It would be shot in slow motion. He was to canter up behind her, then pull alongside and reach for Magician's reins. The first time he tried it, Domino swerved, and Adam almost fell off.

Holly snorted. "Some hero you are."

It took them another half hour, but they finally got it right. Kate was disappointed Liz wasn't back in time to see it all. She'd called again. Her flight was delayed, and she wouldn't get home until nine, maybe even later. By then, it would all be over. At least, Kate hoped it would be. She was getting more nervous by the minute, and it didn't help when the director's assistant ordered her into makeup.

"Do I *have* to?" Kate wailed.

She'd already changed into Tess's jeans and blue t-shirt and figured she was all set to take over her role.

"Yes," Tony Gibson said.

"Why?"

"Because if you don't, the lights and camera will make you look as pale as a ghost." He steered her toward a curtained cubicle at the back of the tent. Holly and Adam insisted on coming with her.

The makeup woman draped a towel around Kate's shoulders, studied her face from several angles, then selected a pot of greasepaint the color of saddle soap.

Ten minutes later, Kate didn't recognize herself.

A thick layer of makeup covered her face and all the way down her neck. Even her ears hadn't escaped. She peered at her alien reflection. There was mauve eye shadow and navy mascara, a healthy dose of blusher on both cheeks.

Then came Ophelia Brown's elaborate wig. Kate tried to ram her hard hat down on top of it, but the black hair stuck out the bottom in defiant little tufts.

Holly giggled. "You look like Bozo the Clown."

"Ronald McDonald on a bad day," said Adam.

Kate wanted to strangle them both. "Just you wait till it's *your* turn," she said, rounding on Adam. But he was laughing too hard to hear.

Aunt Bea came to the rescue. She asked the makeup woman for an elastic, a few pins, and a hairnet, then scooped Kate's wild wig into a neat bun at the nape of her neck and plonked the helmet back on.

"There," she said. "You look just fine."

* * *

Kate jogged down the wide-open trail, determined to look as relaxed and carefree as possible. Magician's ears were pricked forward like he knew they were being filmed. Even the wildlife cooperated. Birds sang and crickets chirped. A squirrel scampered across the path. It was all very natural, almost as if they'd read the script as well. From his perch on a camera platform, Giles Ballantine gave her a thumbs-up. So far so good.

On cue, the motorcycle thugs erupted.

Kate looked around wildly—first one direction, then the other. Pretending to panic, she kicked Magician hard. He bounded forward like a gazelle, the way they'd practiced.

Cameras recorded every move. They seemed to be everywhere at once—on the ground, in trees, and beside all the jumps. At one point, the technicians had laid a dolly alongside the trail so the mobile camera could keep up with her and Magician in real time.

Ahead was the palisade with the motorcycle ramp.

Kate leaned into Magician's flying mane and forgot she was acting. With the roar of the motorcycles behind her, she really was riding for her life. Magician gathered himself up and flew over the fearsome looking jump.

The moment he landed, Kate risked a quick glance back. The bikes were soaring over the palisade like two black-and-chrome vultures. For a few seconds their engines screamed at a different pitch while they were suspended in midair. They hit the ground with a whump and bounced.

"Cut," Giles Ballantine boomed. "It's a take."

After a ten-minute break, he ordered more scenes—long shots of Kate and Magician jumping more fences, close-ups of the motorcycles crashing through the undergrowth—then announced it was time for the first half of the portal scene. The two pines he'd chosen stood six feet apart at the edge of the woods. They were large, ordinary looking trees with twigs and bark—until you got to the other side.

Kate rode between them and gasped.

14

HOLLY KEPT SNEAKING GLANCES at Adam. He looked awesomely cute in his red velvet cloak, black breeches, and white linen shirt. A sword hung from his hips in a leather scabbard, and his boots reminded Holly of the ones pirates wore. They had buckles and floppy tops that folded over. Not great for riding, but definitely cool. Even Domino was all dressed up with red tassels on his bridle and a red cloth draped over his saddle.

Adam yanked off his tricorne hat. "I feel like an idiot in all this junk," he said, scowling at the lace on his ruffled cuffs.

"Wait till you get into makeup," Nathan said.

He'd shown up without warning ten minutes ago.

No sign of Angela. Just him, on his own. Kate was getting changed for her next scene and didn't know Nathan was there. Would she even care? Holly had no clue. Last night at the party, she'd gone very quiet when Angela dragged Nathan into the house. And later, when Holly got home, Kate refused to talk about it.

The tent flaps swung open and out stepped Tony Gibson, looking even more flustered than usual. He ran a hand over his forehead. "She's finally ready."

Behind him, a girl in white floated into view.

Holly blinked. She rubbed her eyes and looked again. Was this Kate McGregor, her very best friend, who clumped around in muck boots and didn't know a camisole from a currycomb? No, it wasn't Kate. It was Ophelia Brown, exactly the way Holly had always imagined.

Her face glowed, her eyes sparkled. Someone had sprayed glitter onto her glorious black hair. Her flowing white gown had long sleeves, a tiny waist, and silvery scarves that shimmered like fairy wings. Holly caught her breath. It was ethereal and magical, and it was absolutely perfect—just like the *Moonlight* cover.

"Wow," Adam said. "Oh, wow."

Nathan let out a long, low whistle.

"You look like . . ." Holly was so choked up that she could barely get the words out. ". . . a *princess*."

* * *

Kate didn't feel like a princess. She felt like a freak—Wedding Barbie meets Lady Gaga. They'd slapped on even more makeup. If she smiled, it would probably crack and fall off. And what was Nathan doing here? Hadn't he gone off with Angela somewhere? He grinned at her, and Kate felt herself blush. But it didn't matter because nobody would see it beneath all the gunk on her face.

"Turn around," Holly said, clapping her hands.

Kate shuffled sideways and trod on her hem. The dress had more layers than a crinoline. She could barely walk in this silly outfit. How was she supposed to ride a horse? And what about a hard hat? Nobody thought of that when they sprayed all that sparkly stuff on her wig. She plucked her riding helmet off the table.

"You can't wear *that*," Holly said. "It'll ruin the look."

"Your mom will murder me if I don't."

"Guaranteed," Holly said, nodding. "But Mom's not here." She snatched the helmet from Kate's hands and shoved it beneath her chair. "Besides, you won't be jumping, you'll be cantering in slow motion."

Kate hated to ride without a helmet, but sometimes you had to break the rules. And Holly was right. Ophelia Brown belonged to the eighteenth century. She'd wear a bonnet or a lace cap, not a USEF-approved riding helmet.

"Okay," she finally said. "Just don't tell Liz."

"I promise," Holly said. "But what about Aunt Bea?"

"Aunt Bea won't say a word," said a voice behind them. "As long as Kate promises not to fall off and bash her head."

* * *

At dusk, Kate rode through the portal. This time it was shrouded in mist. Owls screeched and coyotes howled. Bats swooped among skeletal branches. A giant cat with red eyes looked ready to pounce. It was like being in a Harry Potter film, except she was riding a horse, not a broomstick or a dragon.

Magician chomped on his bit, and Kate suddenly remembered what Holly said about Warrior being a vampire. Would the makeup woman be gluing fangs onto

Magician's teeth? She asked Holly as soon as she got back to the tent.

"That was in the third book," Holly said. "Not this one."

"Phew," Kate said.

"Wanna see *my* fangs?" Adam said. He flashed a hideous grin and drops of something red trickled from the corner of his mouth.

"Oh, man," Nathan said. "That's really sick."

Kate stared at the fake blood. Was Adam's character—Ian Hamilton—supposed to be a vampire? Much to Holly's disgust, Kate still hadn't read the whole book.

"Is that, like, a prop?" she said.

Adam pulled out his Halloween teeth and stuffed them in his pocket. "Nahh," he said. "Just a joke."

"Ha, ha," Holly said. "And here's another one." She handed Adam his tricorne hat. Its red plume stuck up like a feathery antenna.

Adam groaned. "Must I?"

"Get over it, dude," Nathan said. "I did."

"Yeah," Holly said. "If Kate can put up with a wig, then you—"

Tony Gibson bustled up with a ream of instructions. They would begin shooting in ten minutes, and Kate and Adam should get on their horses, like right now.

158

* * *

A fingernail moon danced with millions of stars as Kate cantered across the meadow. In front of her were cameras and giant fans—wind machines, the director said—that rolled backward on tracks as fast as she rode toward them. Kate's hair fluttered in the breeze, her skirts billowed, and a dozen silvery scarves streamed behind her like the gossamer fins of an exotic fish. Magician's feet seemed to barely touch the ground.

Holly's imagination ran wild.

Even though the zombies weren't really there, she could see their deathly faces and smell their rotting flesh. She pictured their ragged fingers reaching for Kate, grabbing her and pulling her down. Then reality intervened. Giles Ballantine gave the signal and into the scene rode Adam. Cape flying like a medieval Batman, he wore a black mask and held his reins in one hand. In the other, he brandished a sword.

Domino's nostrils glowed fiery red, his legs pounded the dirt like pistons. Neck and neck they drew. Adam dropped his sword, then curled his arm around Kate's slender waist, and it looked as if he was about to lift her out of the saddle.

"Cut," the director yelled.

Holly's breath came out in a whoosh. If only Mom could've seen this. Then again, if she were here, Kate would be riding with a helmet and the scene would fail. Holly decided she'd fess up to Mom, but not till she and Kate were twenty-one.

Adam and Kate ran their scene three more times, until the director was satisfied, and each time it got better and more magical. The last shot was so convincing, Holly really did believe Adam was rescuing Kate from evil.

They were both breathing hard at the end of it. So were the horses. Robin and Jennifer threw blankets over their backs and led them away to cool off. Aunt Bea said "Bravo" so many times she sounded like a CD that had jumped its tracks. Sue handed out water bottles.

Kate drank hers down in one go.

A sheen of sweat covered her face. Her lipstick was almost bitten off, her eyes were smudged with fatigue, and she was smiling so hard that her makeup had begun to crack.

She reached for another bottle. "How was it?"

"Absolutely awesome," Holly said.

"The best," Nathan said.

"Really?" Kate looked at him, like she'd just noticed he was there.

"Yeah, really." He winked and gave Kate a thumbs-up.

Holly crossed her fingers. Maybe now, Kate would get a clue about Nathan. But Angela emerged from the shadows and ruined it.

"Nathan," she said, slipping her arm through his. "We have a date. Remember?"

* * *

Kate took one look at Angela's triumphant face, then picked up her skirts and stalked into the tent with as much dignity as she could muster. She ripped off her wig and fumbled for the zipper at the back of her dress. The wardrobe lady stepped in to help and within minutes, Kate was back in her familiar jeans and t-shirt. She was about to peel off her makeup when Holly stuck her head around the curtain.

"You don't have time for that," she said in a loud whisper.

Kate whirled around in her chair. "Why not?"

"Because Nathan's waiting." She grabbed Kate's hand. "Come on, hustle."

"So I can watch him walk off with Angela?"

Holly shot her an evil grin. "She decided not to stick around."

Kate wanted to ask more, but Holly dragged her outside. Adam and Nathan were at the picnic table, pretending to arm wrestle. Nathan gave her a complicated little smile. At that moment, he wasn't Nathan the movie star or Tom the ordinary guy, but somewhere in between. And it made Kate wish she was still in Ophelia's amazing dress. It was easier to be somebody else—a much braver somebody else—when you were wearing somebody else's clothes.

Holly said, "Adam and I are taking the horses back to the barn. Mom's coming up with the trailer."

"She's home?" Kate said.

"Ten minutes ago," Aunt Bea said.

"Come on," Holly said to Adam. She took Magician's reins from Robin. "Let's go and wait for her."

"I'll come with you," said Aunt Bea.

The riding team followed, and all of a sudden it was just Kate and Nathan and a crew of technicians who were loading trucks and taking down the tent. Tony Gibson rushed up and gave Kate a white envelope.

"There's a bonus inside," he said. "For helping Tess."

"Where is she?" Kate said.

"On her way back to California. She said to tell you and Holly goodbye and that she'll be in touch."

"Thanks," Kate said, and stuffed the envelope in her pocket. She was dying to know how much she had made but didn't want to look at her check in front of Nathan.

He said, "What will you do with it?"

"Save it, I guess."

"Nah," he said. "Buy a horse instead."

Startled, Kate looked at him. How did he know what she wanted most in the whole entire world? His green eyes crinkled at the corners, and his mouth slipped into an easy smile. He stuck both hands in his pockets. Something jangled. Car keys? Loose change?

"Do you want a ride home?" he said.

"Yeah, I guess."

It wasn't a fancy convertible like the one Giles Ballantine drove, but a beat-up Toyota, with dents and rust spots, that belonged to Adam's mom. Adam was learning to drive on it, Nathan said.

"That's why it's a trash heap in here," he explained, scooping empty soda bottles, crumpled napkins, and junk mail off the front seat so Kate could sit down. With difficulty, he rammed it into gear and they bumped across the meadow, then onto the dirt road that led down to the barn.

Kate glanced at his profile.

Did she dare ask what happened with Angela? Holly

would. She wouldn't be tongue-tied and feeling like a loser. She'd just come right out with it and ask. But how? What would she say? *Hey, Nathan, did you act like a zombie and chase Angela off?* or *So, what is it with you and Angela, anyway?*

The brakes squealed as Nathan pulled up at the barn.

Kate looked around, surprised. They were here, already? The back of Liz's horse trailer yawned open. No sign of Magician or Domino. They were probably inside being bedded down and fussed over. Okay, so now what?

Nathan leaned toward her.

She stiffened. But he was reaching for the glove box. It fell open with a clang, and a bunch of yellowing maps tumbled out. He rummaged in the mess and produced a blunt pencil that looked as if it had been chewed by mice.

"You got a piece of paper?" he said.

"No."

"Your envelope," he said. "Let me use that."

Kate fished it from her pocket. Nathan scribbled something on the back and handed it to her, not quite meeting her eyes.

"My e-mail address," he said. "In case you'd like to write to me, or something."

All sorts of emotions washed over Kate. She couldn't even begin to sort them out. "Yeah, sure," she stammered and shoved the envelope back in her pocket.

"It's kinda private," Nathan said. "Just for friends and family, so don't give it to anyone else, okay?"

Kate nodded. If she was really brave she'd ask if he'd given it to Angela as well. He probably had, so there was no point in making a fool of herself by asking. Suddenly, the outside barn light came on. Kate blinked and came back to earth with a bump.

He leaned toward her again. This time, he kissed her cheek.

15

HOLLY TOLD KATE NOT TO wash her face. Not ever. That kiss was big. Bigger than California, bigger than the whole world, Holly declared. And a gazillion girls would give their right arms for it, including Angela.

"She's gonna hate you," Holly said.

Kate grinned. "She already does."

They were in Holly's bedroom. It was after midnight, but neither was ready for sleep. Kate stuck Nathan's kiss in her memory bank and scraped off another layer of makeup. One eye was back to normal; the other still looked as if she'd been bruised in a fight.

"Even more," Holly said. "You've got what she wants."

"My check?" Kate said, patting her pocket.

"No, silly. Nathan's private e-mail address."

"She's already got it," Kate said. Angela probably had Nathan's private cell number as well, along with the password to his private Facebook page.

Holly snorted. "She doesn't."

"How do you know?"

"Because she tried to wrestle it out of him."

"When?" Kate said.

"While you were changing," Holly said. "Nathan ignored her about the whole date thing, so she got all huffy and demanded his cell number, then his e-mail address. He told her to visit his web site."

"Nathan Crane the actor dot com?" Kate said.

Holly grinned. "Yup, just like the rest of his fans."

Kate's heart skipped a beat, just like it did whenever she won a blue ribbon. She wanted to jump up and down on the bed, to yell and shout, but that would wake Liz and Aunt Bea. She settled for a small bounce instead.

"Okay," Holly said. "Now open the envelope."

Kate's fingers shook as she pulled out her check. She gasped and looked at Holly, eyes bigger than saucers.

"Two thousand dollars," she said, barely able to believe what she was seeing. "Tony Gibson said I'd be getting a bonus, but I didn't think it'd be *this* big."

Holly whistled through her teeth. "Awesome."

"No, wait, there's another," Kate said.

She slipped a second check out of the envelope. It was for five hundred dollars and attached was a note that said, *Thanks for helping Tess. GB.*

"Twenty-five hundred," Holly said. "Now you can buy half a horse." She whistled again. "And we'd better start looking because it takes forever to find the right one."

But Kate wasn't so sure about that. Maybe she'd already found her.

That night, she dreamed about the old man's horse, except she wasn't a scruffy brown mare. She was a brilliant chestnut with a flaxen mane and tail. She performed elegant piaffes and flawless flying changes and soared over jumps like a big, golden bird.

Just like the horse Kate always wanted.

Don't miss **Book 4** in the exciting
Timber Ridge Riders series. Coming in
December, 2012

Wish Upon a Horse

MORE THAN ANYTHING IN THE WORLD, Kate
McGregor wants a horse of her own, but the
pitiful mare she rescues from the dog-food fac-
tory is hardly the horse of her dreams.

Still, Kate's betting that one day her scruffy
horse will be a champion. Together they'll win
blue ribbons. They'll beat Angela Dean once
and for all, despite the fact that Angela's now
being coached a trainer who's as unscrupulous
as she is.

But can Kate do it? Even her best friend,
Holly, is doubtful, especially when Angela
spreads the rumor that Kate's horse might be
stolen property.

Win the next book

Wish Upon a Horse

Book Four of Timber Ridge Riders

Send me an email at:
TimberRidgeRiders@gmail.com
Put *Riding for the Stars* in the subject line, and I'll
enter your name into a drawing for a free copy of
Wish Upon a Horse

For more information about the series, visit:
www.timberridgeriders.com

About the Author

MAGGIE DANA'S FIRST RIDING LESSON, at the age of five, was less than wonderful. She hated it so much, she didn't try again for another three years. But all it took was the right horse and the right instructor and she was hooked.

After that, Maggie begged for her own pony and was lucky enough to get one. Smoky was a black New Forest pony who loved to eat vanilla pudding and drink tea, and he became her constant companion. Maggie even rode him to school one day and tethered him to the bicycle rack ... but not for long because all the other kids wanted pony rides, much to their teachers' dismay.

Maggie and Smoky competed in Pony Club trials and won several ribbons. But mostly, they had fun—trail riding and hanging out with other horse-crazy girls. At horse camp, Maggie and her teammates spent one night sleeping in the barn, except they didn't get much sleep because the horses snored. The next morning, everyone was tired and cranky, especially when told to jump without stirrups.

Born and raised in England, Maggie now makes her home on the Connecticut shoreline. When not mucking stalls or grooming shaggy ponies, Maggie enjoys spending time with her family and writing the next book in her TIMBER RIDGE RIDERS series.

Made in the USA
Lexington, KY
25 August 2013